Catnaps & Crimes

A Cozy Witch Mystery

Book Store Cozy Mystery Series
Book 2

Lucinda Race

MC Two Press

Editor Kimberly Dawn
Cover design by Mariah Sinclair
Manufactured in the United States of America

First Edition May 2023
Print Edition 978-1-954520-63-9
E-book ISBN 978-1-954520-45-5

Author's Note

Hi and welcome to my world of cozy mystery. I hope you love my characters as much I do. So, turn the page and happy sleuthing .

If you'd like to stay in touch, please join my Newsletter. I release it twice per month with tidbits, recipes and an occasional special gift just for my readers so sign up here: https://lucindarace.com/newsletter/ and there's a free cozy mystery when you join!

Happy reading…

1. Robin's Cafe
2. Bygone Antiques
3. The Pembroke Cliffs
4. Cozy Nook Bookstore
5. Twisted Scissors Hair Salon
6. Betty's Market
7. Old Town Library
8. Miss Judy's Dance Studio
9. The Sweet Spot Baker
10. Bee Bee's Boutique
11. Tuckers Hardware Store
12. The Copper Kettle
13. Police Station
14. Town Hall

Chapter 1
Lily

QUICK NOTE: If you enjoy Catnaps & Crimes, be sure to check out my offer for a FREE novella at the end. With that, happy reading.

I peeked out the front door of my bookshop, the Cozy Nook, right after I heard the nails-on-the-chalkboard kind of grating, but it was metal grinding on metal. A sound that jarred my last nerve. I had spent the last hour trying to perfect a levitation spell, to no avail.

"Milo," I called to my gray tabby cat. "Did you hear that?" If any customer had been in the shop, they'd assume I always talked to my cat like he understood, but in this case, he could. Milo was my familiar.

He slunk into the room. "What are you yelling about? I was having a perfectly peaceful snooze in the sun."

No doubt on the kitchen counter again, but I didn't care. My space was his space. I had come to terms with the fact that we'd be together for life, even if he annoyed me at times. But that was bound to happen in the best of relationships. "There's been a car accident in the town square." I pulled open the door. "I'm going to make sure everyone is okay."

"Right. You want to investigate the scene of the accident."

I glared at him over my shoulder. "You say that like it's a bad thing."

"Lily, you're a witch, not a cop. Leave the mundane stuff to the police. Call your boyfriend, Gage."

I sighed the minute Milo mentioned Gage's name. "He's not my boyfriend. He's a friend who is a man." I slammed the door behind me and hurried over the brick sidewalk to where a late model sports car had veered into a metal flag pole at the edge of the town square, in front of town hall. The driver couldn't have hit that dead center any better if there had been a bull's-eye on it.

A few shop owners and customers had come out of the different stores to see what had happened. From where I was standing, I could see inside the car. The driver was slumped against the steering wheel and on the cream-colored leather dashboard was a fast-growing pool of red. I looked over to Beatrice, who owned Bee Bee's Boutique and Tucker Ross from the hardware store. They were huddled together, pointing, talking, and watching. Jerilyn Busch was just going into the Sweet Spot, and Gretchen Wilson was frozen in place on the sidewalk. All around, locals were milling about, starting their day.

I shouted to anyone who would listen. "Call the police and tell them we need an ambulance. The driver looks to be hurt pretty bad." I refocused my attention on the car and driver. Smoke was drifting up from the engine compartment and I hoped that wasn't a sign a fire was brewing under the hood. I could light a candle but didn't have any idea how to put a fire out. New witch here. I tried the door handle, but the door was locked or jammed. Then I tapped on the glass. Again, the driver didn't move, and I couldn't tell if he was awake. His dark-brown fedora was pulled low, obscuring his face. I ran around the back of the car and attempted to open the passenger door, but I noticed the front fender was jammed back against the door. There was no way I was going to open it.

The wail of sirens was growing closer, and I hoped Gage was coming too. Even though he was a detective and not just a cop, he had a calming influence on everyone, including me. I beat on the driver's window again. "Hey, you need to get out of the car." The wisps of smoke were getting bigger. What if the car burst into flames? The shops nearby could be in danger. I closed my eyes. Did any of the spells I had learned work in this situation? Would the protection spell be effective? So far I had only tried it on my Aunt Mimi when she was the prime suspect in a murder investigation of the former head librarian, and then Gage when the assistant librarian was zeroing in on him after she had a break with reality. She was out to harm Gage and, of course, me too.

In the brief moments I was alone, I tried to decide how best to throw up a protection spell for the buildings and people. Finally, the fire truck, two police cars, an ambulance, and a dark-colored sedan rolled up, all parking at odd angles as if surrounding the scene from prying eyes.

"Gage!" I yelled. "It's smoking." I pointed to the hood of the car.

"Lily, are you okay?"

I was relieved to see his tall, well-built frame headed in my direction. It was sweet. His first concern was for me and not the accident victim, but after what we had been through a few weeks ago with the murder investigation, I surmised it was to be expected. "I'm fine, but the driver is another story." I jabbed a finger in that direction. "I've knocked on the glass, tried to open the doors, but no luck. There's so much blood."

He called to the firefighters and waved his hands in the smoke's direction. "We need the jaws of life and be prepared for an engine fire."

Emergency personnel sprang into action. I moved to the sidewalk, away from the controlled chaos. The whine of machinery pried open the driver's door, and fire suppressant blanketed the engine compartment. I watched as Officers Peabody and Sullivan questioned the group of onlookers, trying to determine if anyone had actually seen the accident happen. I noticed Ross Frederick coming down the street, and when he saw the car, he froze, then hurried in the opposite direction.

Gage had stepped to one side and was on his cell phone. His light-brown hair dipped over his eyes. The worried expression on his face conveyed the seriousness of the situation. Several tense minutes later, the door was yanked from the car.

Two EMTs rushed forward. The first leaned in. I could see her mouth moving, but I was too far away to hear what she was saying. She eased the person back against the seat, then pressed her fingers to his neck and pulled out a stethoscope and placed the round disc against his chest. She leaned in closer and then withdrew. "Detective Erikson?"

Gage held up his finger, showing he'd be another minute. He said a few more words and then put his phone into his jacket pocket. This was the first time I noticed I was chilled to the bone. I rubbed my hands over my arms, all the while keeping an eye on Gage and the person who had checked over the driver. Dang it, I wished I had super hearing or better, a spell that would help me hear conversations at a distance. I'd have to consult my book, *Practical Beginnings*, to see if such a thing existed.

The expression on Gage's face didn't change, but in his hazel eyes, I saw the truth. I could tell the news was grim. He nodded twice. In addition, based on the fact that no one else was taking care of the man, it had been a tragic turn of events, and the car crash had taken a person's life.

Peabody crossed the grass to where I was waiting. Her dark hair was pulled back in a low bun at the base of her police hat. Her uniform was pressed, and her shoes were freshly shined. "Lily. I hear you were first at the scene. Will you tell me what you saw?"

"How are you, Sharon?" She had only been on the force a short while, and as far as I knew, no one called her by her given name except me. She seemed to prefer Peabody.

"I'm fine. Now can you tell me what you saw?" Her words came out clipped, and she held her small notepad out, pen poised, ready to capture my every word.

My eyes stayed on the car, or what was left of it. "I heard the sound of metal on metal. The crash. I ran out and went to the driver's door, tapped on the glass, and asked if he was okay. When he didn't answer and I couldn't get the door open, I tried the other side. Same result. At that point, I heard the sirens, and you all arrived."

"Did you see any other cars, like someone who might have been involved in the crash?"

I shook my head and wrapped my stiff arms around my body. I started to shiver. "No. When I came out, there wasn't even anyone on the sidewalk. It was just the car."

She nodded, jotted something down, and closed her

pad. "If you think of anything else, you'll call the police station?"

Peabody posed it as a question, since I had a tiny bit of a reputation for investigating things I shouldn't. It wasn't really my fault. I loved puzzles and had a burning desire to find the answers. "Of course I will."

She quirked a brow as if challenging the validity of that statement but didn't respond before walking away. The low heels of her dark boots didn't make a sound on the brick sidewalk, and she had her hand on the butt of her firearm, as if keeping it secured.

Gage walked over to me. "How are you doing?"

His tall, muscular frame towered over me, but his height made me feel safe. I shrugged. "Okay." A shiver raced down my spine, as much from the cold as something else. But I couldn't put my finger on what. Possibly my intuition, but why would that be poking at me? This was an unfortunate accident.

Gage slipped his jacket off and wrapped it around my shoulders. "That should help."

I noticed the license plate on the car. Maine. But no one I knew locally drove a fancy sports car. It was impractical with the amount of snow we received each winter. But they could store it and have something else to drive. "Any idea who the driver is?"

"Detective Erikson. A moment, please?" Mac Sullivan, the other police officer, called to him and gestured for Gage to come back to the car.

"Why don't you get back inside, and I'll come over to the shop before I take off?"

I went to hand him the jacket, and he said, "Keep it. I'll get it later."

He was a sweet man, and that familiar pang of wishing

for something, namely Gage in my life, lingered in my heart. "I'll put on some tea."

He touched my arm, and my heart skipped before he jogged to where Mac and Peabody were waiting for him. My gaze went back to the car, where the poor driver was still belted into the seat. The smoke had evaporated, and I figured a wrecker would be called to remove the car. That poor man. I didn't look back as I crossed the street to my shop.

I placed a hand on the doorknob and was about to turn it when I saw Dax Peters striding down the sidewalk. His tall, thin frame had grown downright skinny over the last few weeks. We had met him for the first time when he came into my shop, declaring that Aunt Mimi was innocent of killing Flora Gray. Of course, he was right, but what was he doing here and why now?

I stepped inside the shop and watched from the window. He made a beeline for Gage, Peabody, and Mac. An animated conversation ensued, and Dax strode to the car. He walked around the outside and leaned into the now doorless driver's side. He looked at the driver but didn't move the hat back from his face. Then he seemed to take a long look around the interior before straightening up.

I kept a sharp eye on him. What did he see? Dax looked at my shop. His eyes seemed to bore into mine, and I got the distinct impression he had just told me to keep my nose out of his investigation. A prickling sensation spread down my arms. Investigation?

I knew from watching Netflix crime shows that car accidents didn't warrant a fancy law enforcement person to look into things. It was the local police department that handled those mundane details. The only time they brought in the heavy hitters was when something hinky had been going on.

Gage walked to Dax, and they both looked toward my shop. Gage shook his head, and I hoped he was defending me from this interloper. All I knew about Dax was he showed up in Pembroke, said he had friends in town, and he'd be here for a little longer. But it had been almost a month, and in my book, that was not a short time. Especially since it wasn't tourist season any longer. But there must be something about this accident that wasn't normal. I had to know what it could be.

Milo jumped up on the windowsill next to me. "What did you find out? Someone driving too fast and crashed into the pole?" He began to lick his paw, completely unconcerned for the happenings outside the shop. "Those fancy cars fold like sardine cans." He looked up at me. "You know I've been such a good help mastering a few spells. How about I get a can of sardines as a treat?"

I couldn't help but snort. "It's been three weeks, and I still haven't mastered the levitation spell, so no sardines for you until I do."

He growled like a lion, which I still found unnerving that he could do that. "Maybe my witch needs to spend more time practicing and less time drooling over Detective Cutie over there." He hopped down and trotted off in the direction of the back room.

I didn't have the chance to protest that I didn't drool over Gage, and Milo should really stop calling him Detective Cutie. Where had that even come from? Certainly nothing I had said.

A movement caught my eye. Jill Dilly was running across the town square, her arms waving in the air as she called to Gage. He met her halfway between the car accident and my shop. And she stopped. I could see her chest was heaving as if she had run quite a distance.

I cracked open the shop door and turned my head with my ear directed toward them. With any luck, I could hear part of the conversation, if not all.

"Detective, who was driving that car?" She leaned around him, straining to catch a glimpse of the wreck.

"Jill. We haven't made a positive ID yet, and until we do, we're not releasing any information. We have to contact the family first."

"It's Teddy Roberts, isn't it?"

My mouth fell open, and I snapped it shut before I could burst out a comment that no one needed to hear.

"Jill. When I can tell you something, I promise to call you. For now, please go home."

He gently turned Jill back in the direction she came from. Seeming to vacillate between doing what he said and her wanting to know, he pointed to where her car must be. "I promise I'll be in touch."

Her shoulders sagged, and with a catch in her voice, she said, "I know that's Teddy's car."

Gage looked at me. I didn't care that he caught me listening. He turned to come into the shop, and I opened the door wide. When he came inside, I took his jacket off and handed it to him.

"Before you ask, I'm going to tell you." He gave me a sharp look. "But this doesn't give you carte blanche to investigate."

I slowly nodded. "It was Teddy in the car?"

"It was."

"Poor guy, to die in a stupid car accident."

Gage's face was grim. "Teddy Roberts was dead before he hit the pole. He had been shot."

Chapter 2
Lily

My mouth dropped open, and I snapped it shut. "Teddy Roberts is dead?" I couldn't believe what Gage was saying. "That's not possible, and he was shot? By whom?" I looked out the window at the crowd which had gathered. Peabody and Mac were handling crowd control, and they stretched the heart-sinking yellow tape around the mangled car in a semicircle. Without looking at him, I said, "I didn't hear a pop, just the metal grinding."

"You might not have. I'm assuming the door was closed to the shop, and you were working. Even with sound traveling, you probably wouldn't have heard it. And there is always a chance there was a silencer involved."

He stated it in a matter-of-fact way. I was taken aback. I sucked in a sharp breath. "In Pembroke?" Those little cogs in my brain meshed. "It has something to do with Dax Peters, doesn't it?"

Gage's silence spoke volumes. He turned away and walked in the direction of the back room. "Any chance I can have a coffee?"

He knew to help himself and asking was a way to keep me from diving deeper into my own questions. But the truth of our situation is that wouldn't stop me. Just slow me down for a millisecond. I handed him two mugs from the shelf. One said *Booked for the Weekend,* and the other said *Just One More Page.* The coffee machine sputtered as it brewed the Hawaiian blend I had picked up.

"Smells good." He added cream to our mugs and carried them out front to the wingback chairs near the window. It had an excellent view of what was now the crime scene.

"Don't you need to get out there again?"

He shook his head, and a look of disgust slipped over his face. "Dax took charge. I'm waiting until he needs some help with the locals. Law enforcement types like him drive me crazy." He sipped his coffee. "Go ahead. Ask."

Had he just given me the opening I wanted? I set my coffee on the round table between us. "To be clear, I can ask questions about Teddy?"

He inclined his head. "This doesn't mean I want you investigating, but I figure it's better you ask me directly instead of going around behind my back. We've found that gets you into sticky situations."

That was an understatement. Almost getting hit over the head with a baseball bat was life-threatening. I wasn't about to remind him of what might have happened. In an attempt to get away I threw myself down the stone steps. If my aunt and my best friend, Nikki, who both happened to be witches, hadn't provided me with a soft landing at the bottom of the stairs... I gave an involuntary shudder.

Gage was watching me closely. He knew my moods, and I swore he could read my mind half the time. "If you're not interested in poking around this problem, we don't need to talk about it."

"It's not that. I was just thinking about how I had suspected Teddy of killing Flora and now he's dead. What are the odds?"

He leaned forward, his clasped hands resting on his jean-covered thighs. "I was never clear as to why you thought he was guilty other than he was paying off Flora. Care to refresh my memory?"

"Could that be the reason someone killed him?" This was an entirely different opportunity to see if I could follow the clues and solve the puzzle—well, murder.

"Lily, I just saw that gleam come into your eye, and you need to let Dax solve this one."

I held up my hands as if I were pleading innocence. "I never said I was going to investigate. But if I have pertinent information, I'm going to share it with our favorite lawman, Dax."

"Tell me what you think you know."

He settled into a more relaxed position in the chair. Milo had sauntered out from wherever he had been napping and hopped up in my lap. He gave me a sly wink, and I hoped Gage hadn't seen that. It might be hard to explain. But under normal circumstances, with a cat who wasn't a familiar, they winked just to get something out of their eye. I had nothing to worry about.

"Remember the night I told you Nikki and I went to Teddy's place and we saw him with some man we didn't recognize, along with Marshall Stone and Jill Dilly?"

"The night your house was ransacked and we found Milo locked in a closet?"

Wow. He had excellent recall. That was a month ago. Did that come from his training as a cop, or was it something special about him? Was it possible? No, Gage wasn't a witch even though men could have magic. My dad was a witch, not that we talked about my newfound abilities yet. I still hadn't called my parents to tell them what had happened. I refocused on the present, halting myself from going down the parental guilt path. "That's the night."

His hazel eyes were serious, and his body was taut, as if he was ready to spring into action. His attempt to appear casual by sipping his coffee failed the moment his eyebrow quirked. I knew his tell. Gage was anything but calm. He could wait for an iceberg to melt.

I became a puddle. "I never found out who the other man was with them. Now I'm wondering, is that the case Dax is working on? Do you think the mystery man is involved?" I rose from the chair and got my laptop.

"What are you going to look up? Mystery men who hang out with Teddy?"

I looked at him from under my lowered lashes. He was trying to smother a laugh, but I knew him too well. "It was a man, not men and no, that isn't what I was looking up." Well, he guessed part of what I was doing. But I wasn't about to tell him that. "I was going to see if the town had any special events posted last month. Maybe a stamp collector's convention or something."

Now he laughed out loud. "In Pembroke, Maine? We're known for our seafood festival in late September and fishing during the summer season. We are not the hot spot for stamp collectors."

I could feel the heat flush my cheeks and not from saying something silly, but from the easy conversation with Gage. "Then maybe it was a fishing expedition." I snapped my fingers. "Nate would know that."

"Let me guess, you're going to swing by your aunt Mimi's on the way home just to grill Nate about what might have been happening in town around the time you actively became a sleuth?" He was still laughing.

Before I could answer, the door to my bookshop opened. Dax strode in, glanced around as if he took everything in with one sweep, and crossed the room.

"Detective," he said with a faint Southern drawl. His words acknowledged Gage but his dark, almost black eyes focused on me.

I gave him a customer kind of smile. "Hello, Dax. Coffee?"

"No." He shook his head. "Detective, I need to speak with you outside."

Gage stood and said, "I'll call you later."

I nodded. But there was something unnerving about Dax. He still hadn't looked away.

"Ms. Michaels. You'd do well to remember you are a civilian, and I don't like amateurs mucking up my cases." He gave me a curt nod. "Please and thank you."

The two men left my store. Despite the melodic tone of his voice, I had always been a sucker for a deep Southern drawl; however, I couldn't help but think the visiting officer was very odd. Who said please and thank you in the same sentence after insinuating that I was nothing more than a nuisance? But if it hadn't been for me, Gage would have arrested my aunt for a murder she hadn't committed. I shivered. Two murders in two months. What was Pembroke turning into, the city?

Milo jumped from the arm of my chair to the one Gage had just vacated. "I know that look, Lily."

"What?" To be honest, I still wasn't used to my cat talking and me understanding, but it was getting easier. Especially since he had stopped harping on me to read my personal instruction manual about how to do spells.

"You're going to ignore what that tall, skinny guy said and start asking questions. You'll keep your eyes open and attempt to help Gage."

"He's my friend. Of course I want to help him." Who was I kidding? I'd been in love with this man since high school, but he was clueless. To be fair, I hadn't told him or even hinted at it. I kept playing off that we were best of friends. But there was no way Gage was in the same category as my bestie, Nikki. We had been little hellions running on the beach near my aunt's house from the time we were small. I smiled. Good times.

"I can tell you're thinking about your detective." Milo's voice was a deep rumble which contradicted his cute exterior, soft downy gray fur, and the sweetest face ever.

"You should stop trying to read my mind. You're terrible at it. And I wasn't thinking about Gage. But how much fun Nikki and I had as kids."

"She's a good witch. Can cook fish like no one I know."

And there it was. Milo's snark had come out. It had been hiding for what, three hours? I sighed. "I have work to do, and the first step is to call Nikki. There is a plan to be made about what my next step should be regarding Teddy Roberts and why someone would want to kill him."

"Good luck with that. I thought he'd take off after the last misadventure he had with the law."

That was true. Teddy didn't have family in the area, so why did he stay here? And as far as I knew, his only friends were Marshall and Jill, and she was most likely his girlfriend. Or maybe just a wannabe. I needed my clue board. Since that was sitting in the pantry closet at home, I'd have to go old school with a notebook and pen. I pulled up a stool to the counter where I could see what was happening right outside my shop. Peabody and Mac were still on the scene, but the crowd had thinned considerably.

As I was observing, someone caught my eye. I crossed the room and stood near the wide front window. In case someone was watching, I didn't want it to look like I was gawking, so I picked up a few books and restacked them. It was all for show, and I'd fix them later. Just as I thought. The man from Teddy's dining room table that night was hovering near a bench in front of the hardware store. He wasn't talking to anyone but taking pictures with his cell phone of everything that was going on. Every few minutes he'd lower the camera and turn a degree or two more in the semicircle, capturing every angle.

I continued to watch. Beatrice, Ross, Tucker, and the mystery man were all within hearing distance of each other, but they weren't talking. Which was odd, since three of the four knew each other and all of them knew Teddy.

"Hey, Milo. Come look at this."

He didn't hop onto the windowsill, so I looked at the chair he had been lounging in. Vacant. Just when I needed him to give me his opinion, he had vanished. I turned to watch the crowd again, only this time I had put the books down. My intuition was knocking. I needed to take mental pictures of what was going on. There were clues right in front of my eyes, and I couldn't figure out what they were. At least not yet.

A flash of gray caught my eye. Milo. He was trotting across the street, and I knew he was going to meander through the crowd, picking up on whatever chatter he could. He really was a good familiar, and tonight he might get some of that special kitty milk he loved.

Gage and Dax were standing away from the crowd. I could see their mouths moving, and I really wished I had found a spell for eavesdropping, but so far the book of *Practical Beginnings* didn't have one.

Dax looked up and caught me watching them. He jabbed a finger in my direction. This was becoming a habit, and I could guess he was telling Gage I needed to stay out of this. But I wasn't afraid of some out-of-town cop. It was going to take more than a stern warning. Gage was talking, and Dax was shaking his head. I got the impression Gage was telling him I was good at solving puzzles, and even though he hadn't encouraged me, he also didn't dissuade me either.

Gage's shoulders dropped, and he walked toward my shop. It was then I noticed Milo had been hovering close to the two men. That was fortunate for me. I'd learn firsthand what that was all about just as soon as Gage headed either back across the street or to the station.

Once again, I opened the door and welcomed him in. He pointed to his jacket tossed over the back of the chair.

"I need my coat."

I handed it to him. "Was Dax giving you a hard time out there?"

"Nothing I can't handle." He touched my hand. "Bubbles, do me one favor?"

Every time he used that sweet old nickname, I found it hard to refuse his request. "Stay out of the investigation?"

He nodded. "Dax is right. This time around, I do not know who we're dealing with, and he's not ready to bring me fully into the case. But there is one thing I know for sure." He pulled me into a bear hug. "Whoever killed Teddy wasn't taking any chances. They made sure he was good and dead."

I held Gage tight, wishing I had as much courage to confess my feelings as I had to track down this murderer.

"I'll be careful. And if I stumble across anything, I'll tell you right away and you can tell Dax. This way I'm completely out of it." I took a step back. If I stayed wrapped in his arms any longer, I might just slip up and confess, and not to a crime.

"I can't talk you out of this, can I?"

I gave him a long look. "I will not answer that. It gives you reasonable deniability. If that's even a word."

"It's a word, but the one thing it doesn't give me is comfort."

"Not to worry, Detective. I've got a few skills that I've been keeping a secret from you."

He quirked an eyebrow. "Let me guess. You've been practicing magic."

My stomach flipped. "How did you know?"

Chapter 3
Gage

I laughed at the shocked look on Lily's face with her pretty sable-brown eyes when I teased her about practicing magic. "Don't worry, it's not like magic is real. But it's too bad; you could use a protection shield."

"Gage. Just one time, my house got ransacked." A thoughtful gaze crossed her face as she ran her hand through her short chestnut hair. "You know we never found out for sure who it was, even with all the clues I had uncovered."

I had my suspicions and felt as if something wasn't as tidy as it could have been. But it might be just my being overly cautious when it came to my favorite bookshop owner.

"I've been thinking about everyone who had gathered around, gawking at the scene of Teddy's accident. Do you think the murderer was in the crowd?"

"More than likely. He or she would have wanted to make sure he was dead."

Lily nodded and chewed the bottom of her lip. I knew

that look. Her brain was replaying the scene that had occurred outside of her shop. "What are you thinking?"

"Just that, remember the night I was checking out Teddy's house and he was sitting in his dining room with Marshall Stone, Jill Dilly, and the other man I didn't recognize? What if this resulted from that conversation? Maybe Marshall and Jill know more about this situation than Dax Peters would know being an out-of-towner. We need to tell him. Oh"—she snapped her fingers—"and that mystery man? I saw him taking pictures of the accident earlier."

She headed to the door, and I grabbed her arm. "Lily. He has his way of investigating, just as I do. We're not going to go out there telling him about some man you saw a month ago and then today, but can't identify, and blame him for the murder."

Lily gave me a wide-eyed and innocent look. It wasn't hard for me to soften; her smattering of freckles always took me back to when we were kids and first met. We were so innocent in the ways of the world back then, but she was always ready to solve a puzzle. Not much had changed after all. "I wouldn't blame anyone. However, I would suggest that when he questions Marshall and Jill, since they were good friends with Teddy, that Dax casually brings up the other man."

I shook my head. "No. Just no." I placed my hands on her shoulders, turning her to face me. "You said you'd stay out of this."

"No. I said I would be careful, and I'd tell you right away." She withdrew her cell from her blazer pocket and held it up with a cheeky grin. "I have you on speed dial."

Having me on speed dial was one thing, but for the reason she did was another. I dropped my hands from her shoulders and shook my head. "You better start learning some magic so you can protect yourself when I'm not around."

She stood on her tiptoes and bussed my cheek and then wiped off what I assumed was her pink lipstick. "Don't worry. I'm working on it."

With a promise I'd see her later, I left the Cozy Nook Bookshop and once again surveyed the scene in front of me. Milo came trotting across the grass, and I could have sworn he looked both ways before crossing the street. I rubbed my hand across my eyes and chalked it up to being tired. For a small town to have two murders in just around a month's time, when we hadn't had any for several years, didn't sit well with me. What was happening?

The cat stopped at the door and meowed, so I took a step back and pushed it open, and he slipped inside. Once he was clear, I closed it tight and took one last look before walking in Beatrice's direction. Her shop, Bee Bee's Boutique, had the best, unobstructed view of the metal pole Teddy struck. She was standing outside her shop. Customers lingered on the sidewalk and didn't seem to want to enter any storefront. They were clustered in small groups of three and four, looking around and whispering among themselves. As I approached Beatrice, I gave her an encouraging smile.

I reached her side. It was easy to see she was shaking, twisting a small linen handkerchief in her hands. "Hi, Beatrice. How are you holding up?"

"Hello, Detective Gage."

I smiled despite the situation. She had known me since I was a child, but instead of calling me by my first name or Detective Erikson, she mixed them up. I found it charming, and she seemed to like it. It gave me the respect she thought

I deserved for making detective and serving the people in our town.

"Did you see anything out of the ordinary before the crash?"

"I heard the car backfire and then that awful sound of metal meeting metal. Made an icy shiver run down my spine so early in the day. I came out, saw what had happened, and then called the police station."

I gave her a sympathetic nod. "It must have been difficult. Did you recognize the car or the driver?"

"No, not at first. But afterward, I heard people saying that it was Teddy Roberts. What would he be doing in a fancy sports car? He was a real estate sales associate and not a very good one at that. I don't know the last time he showed a property, let alone brokered a closing." She pursed her lips and shook her head. "His parents were hardworking folks, and when his father passed away last year, I heard he came into a tidy sum. He should have squirreled it away for a rainy day and not wasted it on some fancy car."

I had to wonder if Beatrice knew he had been paying blackmail to Flora Gray before she was killed. But it wasn't my job to speculate or gossip with a potential witness. Getting back to the first part of what she had said, I asked, "The car backfired? How long before the crash did you hear it?"

She thought for several moments. "Pretty close together. Which is why there must have been something wrong with his car to have him lose control and hit the pole."

It was apparent she wasn't aware he had been shot, too. Which lent credence to my idea of a silencer. "If you think of anything else that might be helpful, would you call me down at the station?"

"Of course, Detective."

Before I turned away, I paused. "Is it normally quiet around nine in the morning? I only ask because when Lily came out of her store when she heard the crash, she mentioned the street was pretty empty." I couldn't remember if she had said that or not, but I was trying to see if Beatrice would set the scene for me.

"A couple of people came out of Robin's Café right after I did, but now that you mention it, the only people I saw were Tucker Gleason, who was in front of his store, and Jill Dilly was talking to him." She closed her eyes. "Gretchen Wilson was nearby too."

I thought back to Jill running toward me and thought she came from down the street and not from the hardware store. It had been crazy trying to get Peabody and Mac focused on crowd control. But it was something I'd report to Dax. Maybe Lily had been right about the connection between the get-together at Teddy's and today.

"Thanks again." I made my way down the street to have a similar conversation with Tucker, and I'd swing by Robin's Cafe too. My cell rang, and I pulled it from my coat pocket.

"Detective Erikson."

"It's Peters. Can you meet me near the car? I want you to look at something before it's taken to the garage's locked lot."

I had already started in his direction when on the ground was an empty shell casing. I called to Peabody.

"I need an evidence bag and photos taken of this spent shell. Make sure you get good shots of the location in proximity. Oh, and check for others."

"Detective. Sloppy on the shooter's part to leave behind a brass casing." She withdrew a latex glove from her pocket. Before she could pick it up, Gage reminded her of the photos. Peabody glanced around. "I swept this area before and didn't see it. I suppose I could have overlooked it."

"Or an onlooker had kicked it. Take care and scour the area." I left her standing there, poking around with a perplexed look on her face. She was good, and if she said it hadn't been there earlier, then it wasn't. There were two explanations that sprang to mind. Either it got kicked or dropped in that location. But how to figure out which was the question.

Dax was making notes on his phone. I thought he'd be an old-school cop like me, using pen and paper, but he'd moved to the digital age.

He nodded in Peabody's direction. "What was going on over there?"

"I found a shell casing. Probably from a nine mil. Peabody said she was sure it wasn't there before, but she was going to canvass the area again and get it down for testing."

He gave a curt nod. "Nine mil. Interesting."

I waited for him to elaborate, but of course he didn't. This was one coolheaded detective and not willing to share anything. "When she brings it in, I'll arrange for it to get to the state lab for analysis."

"I'd appreciate it if you'd fill me in on what was going on. I'm concerned more citizens of Pembroke are going to get caught in the literal cross fire."

He gave me a sour look. "This isn't the Wild West. You live in a quaint New England town. Not much happens around here."

Under my breath, I muttered, "Except lately."

"What does that mean?" Dax gave me a sharp look. "Are there other things I haven't noticed?"

"No. But two murders in the span of just over a month

is a lot to deal with. What's next, bank robbers and carjackings?"

His brow arched. "Feeling out of sorts, Detective? Maybe you should get a donut." He pointed toward the Sweet Shop. "And while you're there, ask around and see if anyone saw anything different than what's already been reported."

The hair on the back of my neck stood up. "I wasn't aware I needed to be told how to do my job."

"Neither did I."

He turned his back on me and slowly moved in the direction of the tow truck driver. Clearly, I had been dismissed. Who did he think he was? Yeah, he was a federal investigator, but I still didn't know what exactly he was doing here. Nothing that sinister ever happened this far north. I was beginning to understand how Lily felt when I had shut her out of the investigation into the librarian's murder. But I was a trained police officer, and by wearing a badge, I didn't need to prove my ability. Despite my annoyance, I strode into the bakery and walked up to the counter, noting the shop was empty except one person I didn't recognize sitting by the picture window with a perfect view of the accident and the current state of cleanup.

William North, owner and baker, was working the counter. "Gage, good to see you. Are you here for two pecan cinnamon buns and coffee?" His eyes danced, and he grinned. I guess my secret of being sweet on Lily was not well kept from William.

I had a habit of coming in at least once a week and placing that exact order to take across the street to the Cozy Nook Bookshop. "Where is Jerilyn?"

"She called out today. Something about indigestion. I told her to give the doc a call to make sure it's nothing more serious. But I'm guessing it's something she ate. That woman loves her sugar, and I swear a vegetable doesn't pass her lips."

I didn't want to smile at the correct description, and Jerilyn would be the first to agree with William, so I nodded, indicating I'd heard what he said. "I'll take two pecan rolls if you have any left."

"Business was awful slow today because of Teddy's accident." He withdrew a white pastry box from under the counter and put in two buns and two large frosted sugar cookies before he taped it shut. "Coffee too?"

"Iced, please?"

I didn't need to tell William how we liked them. He set about making them. "So, who do you think offed Teddy?"

That wasn't a word I expected him to say. "What did you hear?"

With his back to me, he shrugged. I wished I could see his expression. It was more telling than his backside. "A few people were talking when I went out, and they said he was dead before hitting the pole." He put lids on the insulated cups and tucked them into a cardboard carrier. "I'm guessing since you're not denying it, it must be true."

"I can't comment. The investigation just started, but when we're through, a full report will be in the Pembroke Edge." I took the carrier and handed him the money. He handed back the change and took a dollar for the tip bucket. Again, just part of the usual routine. I held up the tray and thanked him.

I pulled the door open, and William said, "Jill Dilly was in here before the crash, looking pretty upset. You might want to talk to her next."

"Thanks, William. I appreciate the information, and thanks for the iced coffee. She says all the time you're the only person who knows how to brew it just the way she likes it."

I swear the man puffed up as soon as the words were out of my mouth.

"Always happy to help the courting process, Gage, but dive in. The water is warmer than you realize."

He looked over my shoulder and out the picture window. I saw Dax striding into Lily's bookshop. What was he doing? Forgetting about any more chitchat with William, I hurried back to her shop.

As I walked in the front door, I heard Dax say as he leaned closer to her, "Lily. I was wondering if you could tell me in detail what exactly you saw today. Nothing is too trivial. I've been told you are extremely observant and have a sharp mind to solve puzzles."

If she saw the door open, she didn't acknowledge it. "I thought you'd never ask. Not only did I see a few things today, but a month ago there was something very suspicious that I know Gage was going to tell you. Now that you're here, I'll fill you in."

I didn't like that look in his eye or the flattering tone in his voice. I cleared my throat, and Lily gave me a welcoming smile. "I got here in the nick of time."

Chapter 4
Lily

Gage was wearing a scowl on his face when he walked in carrying a pastry box and a cardboard drink tray. His eyes were focused on Dax. News flash: he wasn't happy the newcomer was leaning on the counter, trying to pay me a compliment. I had Dax's number. He thought complimenting me would get him the information he wanted. Ha! Little did he know I remember the first time we met and how he tried to make me feel like I had nothing to contribute to any serious conversation regarding much of anything. He dismissed me as average.

Milo hopped up on the counter and rubbed his head against my arm. "He is a jerk, you know."

I nodded and scratched the top of his soft head but didn't answer, since talking to a cat when non-witchy people were present wasn't the best idea. They'd think I'd gone around the crazy bend. Which for a short time I thought I had or blamed it on the fact I had fallen and hit my head. I rubbed the knot that remained from the day I discovered I was a witch and wondered if it would ever go away.

Gage set the coffee tray on the counter, and Dax pulled himself to his full six-plus feet. His skinny frame needed the pastry in the box more than I did, but I wasn't about to offer him what I hoped was my pecan cinnamon bun. "Hello. Is that what I hope it is?"

Gage flipped back the top, and my mouth watered. In addition, two frosted sugar cookies with rainbow sprinkles were standing on end in the middle. Dessert for lunch, too. "Thanks." I kissed his cheek and noticed Dax's eyebrows spiking before returning to normal. Might as well give him the lay of the land and let him know that his subtle flirting routine would get him nowhere, even if I was inclined to share certain facts with him.

"Dax, if I had known you were going to be here, I would have picked up a coffee for you."

"After we talked, I remembered that Lily had an excellent view of the street. Instead of waiting for you to ask her questions, I thought I'd get them straight from the horse's mouth."

"Excuse me. I object to being referred to as a horse." I looked from Dax to Gage and didn't disguise my annoyance.

Dax's eyes flickered with amusement. "It was just an expression."

"One that doesn't flatter me or a horse." I didn't bother to offer Dax a coffee from my machine, but took the top off the cup that smelled like vanilla and inhaled. Basically, I shut down that thread of this conversation.

Milo purred, "You put him in his place. Sort of." He stalked across the counter and flashed a look of superiority to Dax before saying, "I have details when they're gone." He hopped down and ambled to a patch of sun washing over the window seat before stretching out. Ah, the simple life of my familiar.

I refocused my attention on the two men standing across from me, one glaring and the other smirking. "Why don't we sit down, and Dax, I can tell you what I saw." If this wasn't a serious situation with Teddy being killed, I'd have to laugh at the two of them puffing up their chests, Gage being all big brother protective and Dax thinking charm would have me spill all the details.

Since neither of them were moving, I picked up my coffee and a cinnamon bun. I was going to sit down and enjoy both treats. I didn't look right or left but settled in my usual chair, which had the best street view. Within moments Gage was in his usual seat next to my left, leaving Dax to sit across from us with his back to the street.

"Dax. How can I help you?"

"I understand you were the first person to arrive after the accident."

This was a rehash of what I had already said, and I knew he had passed the information along. "Yes. I gave Gage a full recount. Do I need to tell you, or has he filled you in?"

He pulled back in the seat, a good sign that he got a tiny verbal smack upside the head, which I found mildly satisfying. Not that I wanted to be obstinate, but there were other details that were more pertinent for this conversation.

"No. Detective, er, Gage filled me in. But you must have a working theory. I know you were instrumental in solving the murder of Flora Gray last month. Although I don't condone civilians getting involved in my investigations like other departments, I would be interested in your thoughts, being that you have a sharp mind. But do us all a favor and don't start investigating."

I wanted to laugh at the way he threw out what he must believe were words to impress me while acting in his official capacity as a first-class bigwig. He implied that Gage had done something improper. I took a bite of the bun and made him wait. After all, it wouldn't be polite to speak with my mouth full.

If he was annoyed with my delay tactic, he didn't show it. I was kind of impressed that he could keep his emotions in check. But that would be a double-edged sword as I might need to know what he was thinking. If he did this question-and-answer thing all the time, it would make my assisting in the investigation much harder.

"You mentioned Flora, and for a while, I thought Teddy was her killer. I was wrong obviously, but he had done some things that didn't add up." I paused for dramatic effect— really to see if Dax was paying attention.

"Such as?"

Gage rolled his eyes at the pandering tone in Dax's voice.

"There was a get-together at Teddy's house. Marshall Stone, Jill Dilly, and a man whom I didn't recognize was there. I overheard them saying that it was a good thing she was dead before they had to make, and I quote, 'more contributions to the Flora Gray retirement fund.'"

Dax leaned forward, his hands clasped as they hung between his knees. "That sounds like a private conversation. How did you happen to hear it, exactly?"

I could feel heat rise in my cheeks. What would he think of me crawling under open windows? Gage had been upset about it. There really wasn't anything Dax could do since Pembroke wasn't in his jurisdiction. "I was crouched under the window. Until my best friend, Nikki Twing, sneezed, and we had to get out of there fast."

If he found my confession funny at all, he didn't react. "You were trespassing?"

I never thought of it in that way. "I guess I was."

"You realize that this conversation couldn't have been used in court if he had been guilty, correct?"

"My listening to a conversation between four people wasn't about proving anything. I was gathering clues in an attempt to help Gage stay focused in the right direction. My aunt found the body, and it was very upsetting to my family. I needed to help." I snapped my fingers. "And Teddy was getting ready to leave town. I think with Jill Dilly, so that is another thread for you to tug on."

"I've known about his plans to leave."

His monotone response deflated me just a bit. "With Jill?"

Dax looked me in the eye. "I'm not at liberty to share that information with you."

I met his look with a challenge of one of my own. "No need. I'll find out. It's just a matter of time."

"Miss Michaels."

"Do you think that will get my attention, Mr. Peters?" With a well-timed cocked brow, I knew he would cave.

"Lily," he began again. "I'm trying to impress upon you this is a unique situation, one last time. A gun was used, and whoever pulled that trigger and arranged for the accident to happen wasn't playing around."

"I've never thought a murderer would be 'playing around.'" I put air quotes around the last two words.

He was still leaning forward in his chair, and he glanced at Gage before continuing. "I'm sorry, Lily. That was a poor choice of words on my part. I know you understand the gravity of this situation."

I placed the bun back in the box and wiped my fingers

on a tissue. "Dax, you've never said what branch of law enforcement you're in. How does Gage know you've been telling the truth? Maybe you're the person who shot Teddy. Ever since you arrived in town, things haven't been exactly normal."

He snorted a laugh. "You're sharp, I'll give you that." He nodded at Gage. "He checked me out." He waited for confirmation from Gage, who instead sipped his coffee and let Dax have the floor. He had a knack for letting people talk about nothing and everything at the same time. Gage always said you could learn the most interesting things when people go on and on in a conversation.

"I'm a fed. And I take special cases that seem to be under the radar. I move around a lot and blend in. I was supposed to come up, keep watch, and take no action unless needed."

That was funny. With the way he dressed in his ironed jeans, perfectly pressed blue shirt, and tailored black jacket, he didn't quite blend in well in a fishing and tourist community.

Milo sat up on the cushion and turned as Dax rambled on with his nonsense.

"You still haven't said what agency." I kept a razor-sharp focus on him, waiting for some sign he was nervous. But he remained silent and looked away.

"Lily, can you describe the man you saw with Teddy and the others?"

If we'd been driving, I'd have a horrible case of whiplash. "I guess you're not at liberty to share the specific federal agency you're with. For now." He might think I was letting him off the hook, but I glanced at Milo. There were ways of finding out what I would need to know, and from what Gage hadn't said, he didn't know specifics either.

"He was balding with tufts of gray hair sticking up, mid-fifties, clean-shaven, and based on his chair height, he was roughly the same height as Teddy."

"Why would you say that?" Dax asked.

"Marshall was sitting at the same time and he's about six five. This man was shorter than that, more like Teddy."

"Can you remember what he was wearing?"

"I only saw him from the table up, but he had on a black T-shirt."

Gage said, "I don't remember you giving me this description."

Before I could respond, Dax said, "He sounds familiar."

He didn't say anything more. Which of course didn't stop me from asking, "Well, who is he?" His mouth set in a thin line, and I knew that look. "Let me guess, you're not at liberty to tell a civilian."

He gave me a side smile. "Correct. But your information has been very helpful. If you can think of, or come across, anything else that you think might be relevant, here's my card."

He handed me a plain white card with black text. It listed his name and phone number. No email or address. I knew from watching Gage when he was handed a similar card there would be nothing on the back. What he didn't realize was any information I might stumble on or discover would be given to Gage. I was loyal, and if there was anything I could do to help him get the recognition he deserved for being a brilliant detective, I was going to do it.

I flashed a sweet, innocent smile in Dax's direction. "I will keep that in mind."

He got up from the chair, and with a curt nod to Gage, left the shop. My gaze followed him. I noticed the street was finally cleared of people and carnage.

Gage attacked his bun like he was a man starving. "I thought he'd never leave."

Placing my hand on the arm of his chair, I said, "Dax is certainly full of himself. He thinks he's clever, but I know he never actually said what agency he works at. Are you sure he's legit?"

"I called the number he gave me to verify his identity, and they confirmed it."

"Don't you think that could be an answering service instructed to relay specific information?" I shook my head. Sometimes Gage was too trusting. "Any chance you have that number on you?"

He withdrew his wallet and handed it to me. I removed my cell phone from my pocket and dialed. After less than thirty seconds, I hung up. "FYI. That number has been disconnected."

"What?" He dialed and hung up too. "So who is he and what's he doing in our town? I'm going to talk to the chief. I'm not comfortable giving him any more information about our investigation into Teddy's murder."

"Speaking of that, let's recap what we know. You're going to solve it without the help of whoever Dax Peters really is." My mouth dropped open. "Gage. Wait. Do you think Dax is the murderer, and he's been in town watching Teddy, just waiting for the opportunity to off him?"

Gage chuckled. "Jumping to conclusions without facts isn't like you. Follow the clues to see what direction they lead in. As for our mystery law enforcement man, I'll do some digging and not to worry, we'll find out who he is really working for."

Satisfied that he was on the case, I polished off my coffee. "Thanks for coming over. When I saw him strolling into the shop, I knew he was here to pump me for information."

"I'm sorry I didn't get here sooner."

He gave me that smile that always made my tummy flip.

Milo hopped up on the arm of my chair. I rubbed his back and he purred. "Lily, did you notice the windshield? The car engine was pushed in from the pole and the windshield was cracked but..."

I sucked in a deep breath and exhaled. "Gage. There were no bullet holes in the windshield!"

Chapter 5
Lily

I was stunned that I hadn't thought of that sooner. Closing my eyes, I recalled the scene of the accident as if it were a photo in my memory. "That means he was dead after the car was in motion and the accident was meant to cover the gunshot?"

Gage looked as if answering me was the last thing he wanted to do. He swallowed hard and gave an almost imperceptible nod. "For the record, I did not answer your question."

"Got it." I jumped up and grabbed a steno pad and pen from behind the counter. Holding them up, I grinned. "In place of the chalkboard. I need to get one for the shop." I laughed at myself when I wondered how many people had an easel chalkboard in their pantry at home. Not many, I suspected.

Before I sat down, I hurried into the back room. I pulled out a fabric mouse from the drawer and sprinkled in some catnip. After what Milo had said, he deserved a treat.

"Here you go, you handsome devil." Gage and Milo

both looked at me as I rounded the counter. I held up the mouse and grinned. "For Milo."

I tossed it on the floor, and he pounced on it. He loved the catnip mouse, maybe as much as I loved chocolate. I chuckled.

"What's funny?" Gage asked.

"Nothing." I wasn't about to tell him what I was really thinking or that they both qualified as handsome. "He's just so darn cute with those toys."

Milo rolled onto his back with all four paws clutching the tiny mouse. In his best tiger growl, he grumbled, "Handsome is a better description."

I sat down and ignored him. Pen poised over the pad, I asked Gage, "What type of crimes get you killed?"

"Love, money, or revenge."

A shiver ran down my back. All three of those might apply, but revenge was the last on my list. Teddy was a real estate sales agent. Not one who'd be caught up in something where revenge was the motive. "I'll bet it is love or money."

"Why?"

"This is Pembroke, so revenge might be low on the list. He was driving a very expensive sports car which puts money at the top of my list. And love is on the table with the triangle of Marshall and Jill still a potential."

"If you're thinking of Marshall or Jill, would they have the compunction to shoot a gun at someone while they were driving by, hoping no one else got caught in the cross fire?"

I wrote down the thoughts as we talked about them. Now on my suspect list, I had:

Marshall

Jill

Bald man

Dax

?

Gage glanced at the paper. "Why did you add a question mark?"

"Well, you know I have a fondness for even numbers. But it's disturbing to think I have an even number of suspects, hence the question mark."

He laughed. "Only you, Lily, would come up with something nutty and make it sound logical." Looking at his watch, he said, "Duty calls. Any chance you want to grab dinner tonight? I made some chili last night and I have enough to feed the town."

"Sounds delish. I'll make cornbread. My house at...?"

"Six?" He filled in the blank.

"Perfect." I tapped the pad. "We can go over my notes, too."

He tugged a lock of my short hair. "I wouldn't expect anything else." He ran his fingers along Milo's side. "See you tonight, old man."

The cat's head snapped up. "Who are you calling old?" But all Gage would hear was him meowing.

After the door closed, I said, "He likes you, so be nice to him."

"I'm always nice to Detective Cutie, but occasionally, his wisecracks hurt my feelings."

That gave me pause. Can a familiar have a tender heart and be very smart? "Try not to listen. It's not like I can say, *hey, Gage, Milo told me he's sensitive, so be careful with what you say to him.* He'd think I was loco."

"Well, I don't. You're a witch who needs to get cracking on some practice. It's like walking for exercise. You only get stronger if you do it every day."

I groaned. "You know I hate any kind of exercise."

"Then think of me like the dentist, and if you don't

brush, or in this case practice your magic, I'm going to have to scrape against your last nerve to get you motivated."

"All right, I'll open the book in a bit, but first you need to tell me what you know about that shell casing."

Milo tossed the fabric mouse in the air and watched where it landed before leaping into the chair that Gage had been sitting in. "Here goes. You saw me taking a leisurely stroll around town. And it is amazing how people will just say anything when they think the masses will never know."

I waved the pen in a circle for him to speed up the story. He held up a paw. "Patience, my good witch."

I hated that patronizing growl of his. I closed my mouth and waited, all the while tapping the tip of the pen on my pad. He looked at the pen and then at me.

"We need to work on your patience. You'll need that in the coming magic lessons. But never mind that for now. As I was saying, I was strolling among the humans when I heard this sound of metal on concrete. There were too many people around to see who dropped them, but it was the shell casings, and not one but two. Of course, this was after the accident had already occurred, so it was an obvious plant from my angle. I heard Beatrice and Tucker talking about Teddy, and they had nothing good to say. Squandering the money his parents had worked to save for him. And one final thing to add to your list, the bald guy you mentioned, he might have been in the crowd earlier."

I nodded. Now we were making progress. "Are you sure? About the bald guy?"

"I didn't see him the night you did, but this guy isn't from here, wearing a black T-shirt and jeans, and he was tall, almost like Tucker. The bald guy was standing close, listening to him and Beatrice talking."

"Now that's interesting. Is it possible he dropped the spent shells?"

"No way to tell. When they were dropped, all I saw was legs."

"Right, but possible." Who was this guy? And the fact he was still in town pushed him up on the list. How could I find out who he was? By taking a run out to the Coastal Motel on Route One A. I could swing by there on the way home.

"I see that look in your eye. What are we doing and when?"

I tipped my head. "Are you sure you can't read my mind? Maybe it's a familiar, witch thing?"

"You forget I spent a few years waiting for you to come into your powers since you took your sweet time opening the *Practical Beginnings* book from your aunt. I know almost every single one of your expressions, and that look that crossed your face means we're going someplace."

I turned the page on the notebook and jotted down *Mystery Man- staying where?* "We're going to swing by the motel on the way home." I got up. It was time to make another attempt at the spell book. Whoever said witchcraft was easy hadn't ever tried to learn spells from my book. I swear it was written in Martian.

"Why way out there? Wouldn't it be better to start at the bed and breakfast places in town?"

"You doubt me? I'm crushed." I laughed. "If black T-shirt guy has been in town for the last month or so, the motel would be the cheapest place to stay, especially since it's after Labor Day. Rates tumble, and you can even work out a long-term rate."

"How would you know that?" Milo got up and made his

way to the counter where I'd be practicing the next spell on my list.

"The B & B in town only drops their rates from November to May. People like to stay in town. The folks who stay at the motel are okay with the seclusion and proximity to the beach in the summer months. But to lure tourists on a budget who still want to come this far north, they make the rates very attractive, so they can't pass up that kind of cost. At least that would be my idea if I owned the motel."

"Logical. That is an excellent skill to have as a witch." He tapped the closed book with his paw. "Time to practice a little magic."

I groaned, but he was right. I needed to work on my candle lighting skill so it came effortlessly, since occasionally it didn't, and then move on to making a feather float. Not that I understood why that was an important skill to master, but it was in the book. Under my breath, I muttered, "I still think I should learn how to fly."

"You need to perfect everything else in the book before we start flying lessons." With a flick of his paw over the cover, the book opened to the candle lighting page. "Now, where are your beeswax candles?"

After my task master, also known as Milo, seemed pleased with my efforts at lighting candles, which I could finally accomplish with a single breath, I was ready to see a customer walk through the door. I had no energy to work on floating feathers. The door over the bell jingled, and I closed the big book and pushed it to one side.

"Hello, Jerilyn. It's good to see you." I smiled at the plump woman with blonde-gray hair as she came in and then seemed to hesitate just inside the door. She was such a sweet person, a bit plain but with kind, pale-blue eyes which were currently hidden by large sunglasses. We had chatted each time she'd come in, and she worked at the Sweet Spot Bakery down the street.

I knew she was a person who loved to browse until she found just the right book, but never was one to come in if the shop was busy. "It's just me and Milo here right now." I gave her a reassuring smile this time.

"Oh, good." She closed the door behind her and came farther into the shop.

"Is there something in particular I can help you find today?" We had a routine. I asked the question. She would shyly shake her head and disappear down the cooking aisle.

"No." She pointed in the direction of the fiction aisle. "Is historical fiction down there too?"

"Yes. That section is organized alphabetically, by author, but I could look something up and tell you where it's located if you'd like."

"I'll just poke around if that's all right with you."

Her voice was so soft I had to strain to hear her. "Take your time. I'll be closing at four as usual."

She dipped her head in acknowledgement and disappeared among the shelves of books. I knew how she felt. There was nothing better than being surrounded by them. I picked up my duster and worked my way around the room, wiping down the windowsills. Not that they were dirty, but maybe I'd catch of glimpse of the black T-shirt guy. I had wiped them all down with zero luck.

I went back to the counter and slipped my book of spells into my tote bag. I would make time to study tonight after Gage left. The sound of crying reached me. I hurried to where I thought Jerilyn would be, but she wasn't in the fiction section but had gone into the children's corner.

I discovered her sitting in a low wooden chair that I sat in for my monthly story hour. "Is there anything I can do, Jerilyn?" I had taken the box of tissues with me before I came down the aisle and handed it to her.

She took a tissue and wiped her eyes. "I'm sorry. I came in to get a new book to take my mind off what happened this morning."

She looked up. With her sunglasses removed, it was obvious she had been crying earlier today. Should I ask why or wait for her to tell me? I thought of Gage and how he could draw out anyone with patience. "May I sit down?"

She nodded and pushed a chair closer to me. After she dried her eyes and blew her nose, she took a fresh tissue. "I suppose you heard about the car accident this morning."

"Teddy Roberts?"

Her head bobbed, and fresh tears appeared. "Uh-huh."

With my voice low, I said, "I heard the crash and went out."

She cried, "We were supposed to be married. Now instead of a wedding, there will be a funeral."

I was glad to be sitting down. That announcement would have me looking for a seat. "I did not know you and Teddy were dating."

Nodding, she sniffed. "For almost a year now. Ever since I sold my parents' house for them. You know, they moved down south to be closer to my brother and his wife."

I hadn't heard that was where they had gone, but I nodded. "It was nice that he handled the transaction for you."

Her eyes grew bright. "He found a buyer so quickly, and they paid cash, too. We accepted a little less than the asking price, but with a quick deal, Teddy told me it made sense to get it off the market so we wouldn't have to pay for lights and heat through the winter. He was so smart that way, always thinking of the little details that would make such a difference."

"Was it after that you started dating?"

"Oh, gosh, no. We started going together a month or so before my parents moved. When he found out what was happening, he offered to handle the listing for us."

Her parents' place was an old Victorian waterfront home that sat on the bluff above the town. It was prime real estate, and they shouldn't have had to reduce the price right away. Could Teddy be into shady real estate dealings and he ticked off the wrong client? I made a note to add that to my list.

Her voice caught as she said, "It's just tragic. We talked about him not buying that fancy car. I told him he'd end up in an accident driving too fast on these old narrow streets, winding around the coast up Route One. But he just had to have it. Said it was on his bucket list to own a sports car and look where it got him. Dead. Just like our dreams for the future." She waved her left hand and there was quite the rock on a very important finger. "He gave this to me last night, and we were supposed to go to the paper today and put the announcement in for next week. The wedding was going to be in June. After all the years of waiting, I was going to be a June bride."

She let out a shaky sigh. I felt so bad for her. As Jerilyn continued to talk about the car accident, I realized she didn't know someone had shot him and I wasn't about to tell her.

"Why didn't you come with Teddy to movie night at the library?"

Her eyes met mine. "We were waiting for the right time to let everyone know. Teddy thought it might hurt his business reputation since he sold my parents' house and all. We decided to wait a year before going public. Now we'll just be a part of the gossip mill, and I'll become poor Jerilyn. The Pembroke spinster." She got up from the tiny chair. "I'm not really feeling much like reading. I'll come back another day." She placed her hand on my shoulder. "You understand, don't you, Lily?"

"Of course. Whenever you're ready, there will be plenty of books for you to choose from."

She straightened her shoulders, wiped her eyes one last time, and hurried from the shop.

Milo came around the corner. "And just what are you going to do about that?"

I stood up and glanced at the closed door. "My suspect list just got a new name."

Chapter 6
Gage

Later that night, when I approached Lily's house, the front porch light clicked on. I smiled at the welcome. It was as if she always knew when I was going to pull into the driveway. It felt good. I thought about what William had said earlier today. Was I wearing my heart on my sleeve when it came to her?

The back door opened, and I saw her head peek around the corner of the door. "Gage, are you going to sit there all night or come in?"

I waved and pushed open the door. "Sorry. I was lost in thought for a minute." I went around to the passenger side and got the cast iron Dutch oven from the floor. "Chili is piping hot."

She held the door wide, and I walked into her kitchen. It was cozy and inviting, and the table was set for two. "Spice wise or just temperature?"

"Both." I chuckled. "Cornbread smells good and do I also smell dessert?"

With a laugh, she closed the door and gestured for me to put the oversized pot on the stove. "Nikki called and said to swing by her place on my way home. She was making gingerbread and fresh whipped cream and you know I can never refuse her desserts."

"Me either. I'm still hoping one of these days you'll fix me your specialty." I wanted to lean in and kiss her cheek but held back. The moment had passed now that I was inside. I usually tried to do the glancing kiss when I entered her house and on my way out the door so it was all casual like. My next chance would be when it was time to leave, and I would not rush that.

She waved her hand over the towel-covered baking pan. "I did. It's called the Nikki special." She laughed. "You don't want me trying to bake. The smoke alarm goes off, the center is never cooked, and I've been known to leave out a key ingredient a time or two."

"It can't be that bad." I turned the burner on to make sure the chili was steaming when we were ready to eat.

"You were talking about magic earlier. Well, that's Nikki's talent. I'm still figuring out what my specialty is."

"I'll keep that in mind." I looked around, expecting to see her easel which she called her clue board.

"Looking for what I was up to after you left the shop today?" Her brown eyes sparkled with that irrepressible mischievous streak.

"I thought you'd have it out so we can discuss it over dinner."

"Not tonight. We're changing things up. We'll have dinner and then review the clues over dessert in the living room. I'll share what I've learned so far."

"Come on. That's not fair. You're withholding evidence from a detective."

Her eyebrow arched, and she crossed her arms over her midsection and popped out her hip. Oops. Now I had done it. I was always withholding something from her when it came to my job.

"Really? You want to go there?" I could almost hear the tapping of her foot. I looked down and her sock-covered foot wasn't moving. Yet.

"I'm sorry I couldn't tell you everything about your aunt Mimi last month. I was doing my job."

She gave me an assessing look, as if trying to decide if I would ever be off the hook. "I know. But you're so fun to tease."

I wanted to remind her I was a sworn officer of the law, but instead, I laughed. "You're incorrigible, and I love it."

She dropped her arms and stood straighter at the word love. It wasn't like I had said I love you and shocked her, but I guess using that word in conjunction with me and her was too much. My next question came out like a croak. "Did you get sour cream and shredded cheese for the chili?"

"And chopped onions and jalapenos." She opened the refrigerator and began handing me small dishes with the extra toppings and I was happy about the change of subject. Even though things should have been tense between us now, it wasn't. We fell into our simple rhythm of two old friends who've had dinner together countless times over the years.

"So, did you decide to ask Aunt Mimi's lawyer, Jordan King, on a date?"

I took the ladle from the drawer next to the stove. "No. Why?"

"She looked like she wanted you to. I saw the way she was leaning into your personal space."

I gave Lily a sharp look. There was a tone I'd never heard before in her voice. Could she be a tiny bit jealous? "No. It was all case related and besides, she has a reputation as a barracuda in and out of the court. I don't think I want to put my boat in that water."

With a curt nod, she picked up our bowls, and I filled them to the brim. We sat down with the basket of cornbread between us.

"Have you gone out with anyone recently?" I held my breath. I didn't really want to know, but then I did.

"No. The only new person I've met in ages is Dax, and he's not exactly my type either."

That was a relief. "What if he asked you out? Would you go?"

She paused for half a moment. "No. I'm waiting for the right man to come along. I'm in no rush."

I slowly let my breath out. "That's how I feel too. When the time and girl is right, I'll know it."

She looked at me, opened her mouth, and then closed it as if she had changed her mind on what she wanted to say. "I forgot the butter for the cornbread."

Once again, I wanted to kick myself. I could have said something like I've found the right girl, and she was sitting across the table from me. But nope.

A little while later, we had cleaned up the dirty dishes, and we each had a heaping bowl of gingerbread and whipped cream as we walked into the living room. There was the clue board set up, and Lily had draped it with a lavender sheet.

She saw me glance at it and picked up the edge. "After the last time it was erased, I don't take chances. I keep it covered or out of sight from anyone who might decide to come poking around."

I had to laugh. "This from the woman who sneaks under open windows to listen to conversations?"

"What can I say? I do what works in both instances." She lifted the sheet and dropped it on a side chair before turning on the lamps and facing the board toward the sofa. I sat down next to her.

"You've been busy. A list of suspects and I see you added a name, so you're back to being uneven again."

"I can fix that." She got up and, using the edge of the sheet, erased the question mark from her list. "Back to odd numbers again."

Oh, her loveable quirks. In the second column, she added information about the motel outside of town and there were two names listed there. Dax Peters and Jake Morrow.

"Who's Morrow?"

She beamed like a kid who had all the answers in math class. "Meet black T-shirt guy, Jake Morrow, and he's staying at the Coastal Motel. And guess who else is staying out there?"

Before I could answer her, she announced, "Dax Peters."

"That I knew." I spooned a large portion of cake into my mouth and the whipped cream was flavored with a hint of cinnamon. Lily was right, baking was Nikki's calling.

"Good, right?" She pointed to my dessert bowl.

"Yes. Let's stay on track. I want to know more about what you discovered."

"All right. Jake Morrow has been staying at the motel for over two months. He paid in cash and up front for three months. I talked with Monica Webster. Did you know she bought the motel from old man Wright last spring for a great price? And guess who was the sales agent?" Without giving me a chance to answer her, she said, "Teddy Roberts. But that's not part of the story. Morrow told Monica that he was here getting reacquainted with his long-lost cousin, and no, he never gave a name of the cousin."

"Okay, so you hinted you think there is something off about the real estate deal. With Teddy as the agent?"

"Yes," she exclaimed, "and guess who else's home sale he handled?"

"A decent portion of Pembroke." Her smile dipped before going wide again. "Yes, but there is something different about this one. He sold Jerilyn Busch's parents' house. They took a lower amount than asking for a quick sale. You and I both know that house was worth a small fortune. Even if it wasn't in great shape, that location is worth a million bucks."

"What did it sell for?" I knew she'd have the figure, but now I was afraid of the answer.

"Seven hundred thousand. And the house is beautiful. Move-in ready too."

My mouth fell open. "You're kidding, right? Talk about money left on the table."

"Oh, but there's more. Guess who got engaged last night? And I saw the sparkler on the correct ring finger."

I shook my head. I didn't know where this was going.

"Jerilyn and Teddy. She was in the bookshop today and told me they had kept it quiet. She said they didn't want anyone to get the wrong idea about that business deal. And I can top that. She never mentioned that a gunshot had killed him, and I didn't tell her."

Lily sat back, pleased with her news, and to her credit, most of this I hadn't uncovered. But there was one tidbit I could clear up. "I knew Dax was staying out there. And the long-term rental fees would be lower than staying in town. He said it also helps him keep a low profile around town."

She laughed. "If he wants to blend in, he should start to

dress more like a local. The clothes he wears make him stick out like someone from the city."

"In his defense, he's probably from DC or New York."

Lily actually rolled her eyes. "Puh-leeze. He's got you eating out of the palm of his hand. I'll bet you don't even think there's a potential for him to be a suspect. Have you forgotten that number he gave you to verify his identity has been disconnected?"

"No, but maybe it's protocol. How would I know? I didn't find out a thing when I talked to the chief." I couldn't believe we were arguing over Dax Peters.

With a wave of her hand, I stopped talking as her eyes went wide and she stared at me. I couldn't imagine why she was shocked that I would stop going over the same topic, especially when it came to a man like Dax. I saw the way women in town looked at him. He was a good-looking guy and if I was reading the situation correctly, it was only a matter of time before he asked Lily out on a date.

She glanced at Milo, who meowed, and her chin dipped. "There's no sense arguing about Dax. But there is a lot to unpack when it comes to real estate transactions that Teddy was involved with and how much money he made off them. How else could he buy that car? And you should see the ring that Jerilyn is sporting. It's got to be well over a karat."

I pointed to her board. "You need to add all of this. It's good stuff. But I would prefer you don't go back out to the motel in search of Mr. Morrow until I can run down some information on him. With any luck, someone will mention having a cousin in town visiting."

With a clap of her hands, Lily said, "I'm going to guess that Teddy Roberts is that cousin. Maybe not, but he was at Teddy's house. I'm going to have to talk to Marshall and Jill.

But how do I tell them what I saw without confessing I was lurking?"

"You don't. Take that item off your board. How about you go to the town hall and check out real estate transactions?"

"Why? I can do it all online. No need to sit down there. But," she said slowly, "I might pick up some interesting tidbits as people come and go." She beamed. "Sometimes, Gage, you're a genius."

Her willingness to go to town hall had me concerned. She was right on one point; there would be many people coming and going, and with the recent death, gossip was going to be plentiful.

"I think I'll set my phone to record everyone. That way, I can listen to it later and see what I can learn."

I shook my head. "Absolutely not. No recording devices. It's downright crazy. If the murderer is there and discovers what you've done, you could get into far more trouble than you bargained for. Stick to listening if you have to go down there at all."

"Okay. I won't record anything." Lily finished making notes on the chalkboard and stepped away, then drew lines from her suspects to possible motives.

I heard a car slow outside her house, nearly stopping, followed by a soft humph. With the blinds open and the lights on, we were sitting ducks. I grabbed her by the hand and pulled her away from the window. "Get down!"

Chapter 7
Lily

Lying next to Gage with half his body covering mine, glass rained down on and around us. "What the heck?" I struggled to get up, but he shushed me. What he was waiting for, I wasn't sure.

A couple of minutes after the glass stopped showering us, he eased off me and asked, "Are you hurt?"

I checked my arms and patted my face. "I don't think so." A thin trail of blood was trickling down his cheek. "But you are."

"Never mind. I'll be fine. I need to call this in to the station."

After we got up off the floor, I saw the blood was more than a trickle. I sat him down in a ladder-back chair. "Stay put. I'll get something to clean your cuts. You can call the station from there."

Frozen in place, I looked at the bay window. It was smashed. A large rock lay on the opposite side of the room. Who would have felt the need to throw something through a window? And Gage had gotten hurt protecting me. Nausea slipped around my insides when I thought of what might have happened. My knees trembled, but I wasn't about to let Gage know this had shaken me. I touched his arm above where his shirt was ripped by either glass or the fall. "Be right back."

He grabbed my ice-cold hand and squeezed. "Are you sure you're not hurt?"

I kissed his cheek, lingering there to reassure myself he really was okay other than some minor issues. "My hero saved me."

Color flushed his cheeks, and I hurried from the room. Once he couldn't see me, I leaned against the wall and took several deep, shaky breaths. This morning seemed like a lifetime ago, but obviously, someone thought I knew something, even if I didn't realize it. Yet. Once I had composed myself, I gathered antiseptic, bandages, a wet washcloth, and tweezers. I hoped there wasn't any glass, but just in case I needed them, they'd be at the ready.

As I entered the room, Gage was saying, "That's right. I need Peabody and Mac at Lily's house. There's been an incident."

He put his phone away and looked up when I asked, "Ready for Nurse Lily?" I forced my voice to be bright and wished I had some magic to heal the cuts. Then my heart stopped. Where was Milo? If he was okay, why hadn't he rushed into the living room at the sound of glass breaking?

"Gage, I need to check on Milo. Give me a minute?"

Concern filled his eyes. "I'll help you look. Where was he the last time you saw him?"

My heart pounded in my chest and now my breathing came in fast gulps. "What if he's hurt?"

"Shh. We'll find him. I'll bet he's sleeping in your office. You know how he loves to disappear all the time."

I nodded but was afraid something awful had

happened. "Milo?" I called. "Milo!" I waited to hear the little thumping sound he made as he scurried to wherever I was. But the house was deathly still. I flung open the back door and as loudly as I could, I called for him. Walking across the back deck, I continued to yell as loud as I could.

I clutched the cool black tourmaline with the amethyst pendant of protection that Aunt Mimi had given me when I learned I was a witch and he was my familiar. It grew warm in my hand, and I closed my eyes and concentrated on the following words. *Milo. Come home. Milo. Come home. Now.*

The pendant grew hotter, and it burned my hand, but I wasn't about to release it. The magic would never hurt me. My protection spell was about pure love. I repeated myself again. Gage was at my elbow, but he never asked what I was doing. Instead, he cupped his hands around mine and held on. If he felt the heat building, he never said a word.

Anguish filled my heart. "Milo, I need you. Please come home." For several more minutes, Gage and I stood, my hands clasped over the pendant. Waiting.

"Lily. Open your eyes. Look." His voice was soft.

I did as he asked. First one and then the other. There was my gray tabby strutting up the driveway. Unscathed. I scooped him up and smothered him with kisses. "Where have you been?"

"Snooping." He wriggled in my arms. "What's up with you? Have you been enjoying my catnip?"

I laughed, but I didn't answer him exactly. "I was worried you were hurt. Someone hurled a stone through the front window. But I can see you're okay." I kissed him again and set him down.

Gage ran his hand along Milo's back. "Good thing you were out roaming, little buddy." He picked Milo up. "I'm going to carry him, so he doesn't step on any slivers of glass."

If Milo had been an ordinary house cat, I would have done the same, but he was smarter than some unmagical people I knew. But I was grateful that Gage had thought of it.

"Come on. Let's get inside, and I can take care of you next." I glanced over my shoulder as the sound of the police siren grew closer. "The cavalry will be here soon." I had to wonder if Dax would be far behind.

Chaos was the only word I could think of as Peabody and Mac took pictures of my living room, the house from the street, and even pictures of Gage's back, which unfortunately had several large but superficial gashes.

"Ouch." He flinched and almost stood up from the chair. "What are you using back there?"

"Stop. It's just a washcloth with warm water to wash the blood away."

Milo was hovering in the doorway and carefully picked his way over to me. "I got a message to Mimi. She's on her way with salve for his back."

Gage reached around and picked Milo up. "If you're going to torture me, I'm going to keep Milo safe."

It sounded a tad unreasonable, but who was I to argue? "Makes sense to me." Knowing that Aunt Mimi would be here soon caused me to slow down what I was doing. I was positive her salve would promote healing quicker and with less pain than the brown bottle I had on the side table.

"Detective?" Peabody was standing in front of him. "Glad you're alright."

"Thanks, I know you and Mac were off duty but I wanted my best team on this investigation. Is Jonesy on his way over too?"

"No, he and Shepard had a call at the motel, and when I heard on the radio it was Lily's place, Mac and I needed to be here. Besides, we're happy to pull a little OT. Also, I've got one of those feelings you say I need to follow."

"And what's that, Sharon?" I asked.

"I think this is related to the accident this morning. The last time your house was ransacked, it was when Ms. Gray died. We still don't know who did that. When I called Mac, he agreed and said he thought the same." She shrugged. "Besides, it's the detective. We had to put eyes on him."

From the corner of my eye, I saw Aunt Mimi hurrying up the front walk with Nate, her new husband, at her side, carrying a large tote. Behind them was Dax Peters. Too bad I hadn't placed a bet with someone. I knew that man would show. Tonight, he was wearing exactly what he had been wearing earlier. And he still looked freshly pressed. How did that man do it? Once I ironed and got dressed, the wrinkles came back even faster.

Mac held the door for Aunt Mimi, Nate, and Dax. She picked her way over the mess to inspect Gage's back before she spoke. One glance at me said it all. She was not happy, but then again, she was relieved we were okay. So much was said between us without words. She kissed both my cheeks and placed a comforting hand on his shoulder.

"Gage. Is it okay with you if I put some of my special cream on your back? It will take away any pain you might have and promote healing. It's all natural."

He looked back over his shoulder and smiled. "Anything has to be better than what Lily's been using. I've wanted to hop up from this chair three or four times already."

She gave me a disapproving look. "Are you still reading the book?"

I wanted to scream. Who had time to read a book that had hundreds of pages, learn the spells, and then perfect them so my magic would work properly? "I'm getting there, but there are a lot of words on every page."

"Milo will help you."

I tipped my head in Gage's direction, who was now chuckling.

"What's in the book and what's this little bundle of fur going to do? Sit on the pages and hold them down?"

Aunt Mimi wriggled her fingers in Nate's direction, and he handed her the tote. He stood in front of Gage as he stuck his hands in his front pockets, and he said, "Don't ask, except to know that Mimi has given Lily all her special recipes, so the next time you two get into a pickle like this, Lily will take care of it without resorting to drugstore medicine."

Gage nodded. "Good to know." He craned his head around to look at me. "Get crackin' on that book. With the way our luck is running, we'll need whatever you can mix up."

Great. Now I had one more person with my familiar telling me to read the darn book. "I'll jump right on that after I fix the window and clean up this mess."

Nate volunteered to sweep up the debris. "I brought over a couple pieces of plywood to nail over the hole for tonight. Tomorrow I can run to the lumberyard and see if they can quickly get a replacement in for you."

I smiled my thanks to him. At least there was one person who wasn't harping on the darn book. For all I knew, there was something in there to fix the window, too.

Dax had walked around the room, bent down to examine the rock, and looked at me and Gage. "What were you doing when this happened?"

I placed my hand on Gage's shoulder. "Enjoying dessert." I nodded toward our forgotten bowls. "Gingerbread and whipped cream. I have some in the kitchen, if you're interested."

He frowned. "That's all?" He noticed the chalkboard easel on the ground. "What's that?"

Thank heavens the side he was looking at had been smudged. "I write things on it for my bookshop. You know, a sidewalk sign for sales and specials." Internally, I prayed he wouldn't turn it over and see what I really wrote on it.

He gave a curt nod and stepped over it. "When the officers are done, you can go ahead and clean this up. Detective, I'd like to talk to you first thing tomorrow in your office. Understood?"

The hair on the back of my neck stood on end. I wasn't scared of him, but the tone of his voice grated on my nerves. As if Gage was going to run amok with a new tidbit that Dax had overlooked. But it confirmed one thing without anyone saying a word. This must be related to whatever Dax was investigating and Teddy's death.

"See you at eight, Dax."

I looked between the two men. "Do you want me there too?"

In unison, they said, "No."

I huffed. "Nice way to tell a girl she's not wanted."

Aunt Mimi broke the tension by pronouncing that Gage's cuts were cleaned, medicated, and bandaged. "And Gage, one had a sliver of glass, but I'm sure I got it all. If you swing by my house tomorrow, I'm happy to take a look."

Gage put Milo on the seat of the chair and pulled his tattered shirt down his back. "Do I need to see a doctor?"

"I'm sure that won't be necessary, but of course if it makes you feel better." Her voice trailed off.

Nate said, "Mimi takes care of all my injuries from the

boat, and you can just imagine how many that is. Trust me, she's better than the doc with this kind of stuff."

Gage gave Mimi a hug. "Nate's word is gold for me. I'll swing by around lunch if that's okay with you?"

She patted his cheek like she had when we were kids. "I'll have lunch."

He started to protest, but she put a hand up. "And I won't take no for an answer."

"Aunt Mimi, what should I bring?"

Her brow arched, and she laughed. "This is lunch for two, not three." And then she gave me a sly wink.

Oh, what was she up to now? I shook my head.

Mac came in from the front yard. "I think we've got all we need. Lily, can you stop in tomorrow and give your statement? I know Gage was here, but you have a good way of seeing things."

"Thank you, Mac." I grinned at the people standing in a semicircle around me. At least someone thought I could add value to the conversation. "Will nine be too late?"

"Not at all." He nodded to Gage. "Peabody and I will take off now. See you in the morning."

"Thanks for coming out tonight." Gage shook hands with both of them. It was easy to see not only did he enjoy working with them, but the respect they had for each other was deep.

"Is it okay if we clean up now?" I asked the question but didn't direct it to any one person.

Peabody put the rock in an evidence bag. "I'm good here." She turned to the front door and said good night to my aunt and Nate before going out. I thought it was curious she didn't acknowledge Dax. When Mac did the same, the vibe I caught was one of distrust. Not that they weren't professional, but it was awkward.

Dax was next in saying, "See you in the morning, Detective." He nodded to Aunt Mimi and Nate before turning to me. "If you need anything, Lily, you know how to reach me." He marched out the door without a backward glance.

What the heck had he meant by that? If I needed a law enforcement person, Gage was my go-to guy. Second and third on the list were Peabody and Mac in that order. I could feel eyes on me, and when I looked away from Dax's retreating frame, it was Gage who was staring at me.

"What do you think he meant by that?" I asked, feeling heat flush my cheeks.

Gage looked out through what was left of my front window. "There is only one explanation. Does the phrase *keep your friends close and your enemies closer* ring a bell?"

"Which do you think he is?"

"Lily, that's up to you. But be very careful around him. After tonight, I'm not sure he can be trusted."

"What makes you say that?"

Gage slipped an arm around my shoulders and pulled me close to his side. "No one called him about what happened."

My mouth gaped open. "So how did he know?"

Chapter 8
Lily

The next morning, I strode into the police station, exhausted. The entire night I kept seeing the car accident in my mind. I wasn't any closer to figuring out what happened, what I saw, and why someone would hurl a rock through my front window.

I smiled at the clerk sitting behind the desk. "Hi, Alice. Can I go down to Gage's office?" The young lady would always look like a pretty china doll, with her long blonde hair, big round blue eyes, and pert nose. It was a little disconcerting. She always looked perfect without a hair out of place.

"Hi, Lily." Her voice matched her appearance—perky. "He said to go in as soon as you arrived."

I entered his office, and Dax was sitting in an unforgiving wooden chair across from Gage's desk. At least the man hadn't commandeered Gage's office like he seemed to take over everything he could.

"Good morning." I made sure to add an extra-wide smile in Gage's direction.

Dax stood and offered me his chair. At least the man

had manners. But I politely declined. "I'm here to check on Gage and to give you this." I withdrew a couple of typed pages. "My notes from yesterday and last night."

Gage flicked a triumphant smile at Dax. "Detailed to a fault." He took them and skimmed what I had documented before passing them to Dax.

"Other than what's there, I have nothing else to add." The words rang hollow when I didn't finish the sentence with *for now*. But Gage knew me. There was no need to rile up Dax with the idea that I was going to be checking things out today. "If you don't need me, I have to get to the bookshop."

"Lily." Dax's low tone stopped me before I could leave. "Will you be at your shop all day?"

I darted a glance at Gage before I looked at Dax. With a lift to my chin, I smiled. "Of course. I have a business to run."

Gage hid the smile that appeared on his face by picking up his coffee mug. But I saw the twinkle in his eye, and we both knew I was going to research, peer out my window, and make plans for my next move.

Holding the papers aloft, Dax said, "Thank you for bringing these down. I'm sure they'll be useful."

Reminding Gage to stop at the store after he saw my aunt for lunch, I left. I detoured to the town hall to see what I could find out before I had to open the bookshop. I glanced at my watch, seeing I had just about an hour.

I turned the key in the door. The old brass lock turned easily. A burst of pride filled me when I entered the sunlit space of the Cozy Nook Bookshop. It might be a hand-me-down bookstore from Aunt Mimi, but over the last couple of years, I had made it mine. By adding the window seats and coffee machine as my contributions to this thriving shop, I encouraged customers to sit and relax. Milo was stretched out in the sun on the muted oriental carpet. He must have used the kitty door I had installed in the back door when I adopted him.

Aunt Mimi had always preferred to bring her familiar Phoenix, a traditional black cat, to the shop in a carrier. Once Milo revealed he was my familiar, the carrier went by the wayside and now he rode with me occasionally, but more often than not did his own thing.

I flipped open the closed sign and turned on the overhead lights. Milo opened one eye so he could see me from the slit. "Did you find out anything interesting?"

"Let me get settled, and I'll tell you everything." I stored my tote under the counter and hurried into the back. Once my lunch was in the refrigerator and the coffee pot on, I stashed a new catnip toy in the drawer. The bell on the front door jingled, and I stuck my head out to see who had come in.

"Jerilyn. This is a surprise." I could see she had been crying and probably for most of the night. Her eyes were red and bloodshot, and her face was a blotchy pink.

"I didn't know where else to go."

"Why aren't you at work? Staying busy will help you keep your mind off things."

"I couldn't go in today." She flopped into one of the wingback chairs and sniffled. I handed her the box of tissues from the counter.

As she dabbed her eyes, she said, "I'm still in shock."

I sat on the edge of the other chair, curious about why Jerilyn would come here. We weren't friends. She was always friendly when I popped into the Sweet Spot, but that was as far as it went. Heck, until yesterday, I never even thought she had a life other than her job. Shame on me.

"I understand." I looked at Milo, and if a cat could shrug, he did. "Is there anything I can do for you?"

She shook her head and loudly blew her nose. Most unladylike. "I contacted his cousin, and he acted like he had never even heard of me."

"Oh?" I sat a little straighter in my chair. "What did he say?"

"I told him I wanted to plan the funeral. Have it in town next week."

"He didn't like that idea?"

"Tommy, that's his cousin, said Teddy would be cremated, and according to Teddy's last wishes, he wanted to be scattered over the ocean."

She dabbed her eyes with what was surely a damp tissue. But who was I to judge?

"You can still hold a service like you wanted to." I deliberately kept my tone gentle because of her obvious state of mind, but also, she might say something else that would prove useful to my investigation.

"Nope. He said I will not be involved. I quote, *I don't want some so-called fiancée mucking things up for me,* end quote." She looked at me. "What should I do? Call a lawyer to stop him?"

I took her hand and said, "Do you know if Teddy had a will?"

She nodded. "He used a lawyer in Portland. I have his name at home."

"That is the best place to start. See what his wishes were. As his future wife, he may have arranged for you to have some voice in what happens next."

Her face lit up. "Do you think so?"

I nodded. "Yes, you were starting a new life together. You can let his cousin know if you think it would be a good idea. You could check with Gage on when his..." I hesitated to use the word *body*.

"Remains." She gulped. "That sounds cold and heartless." She tapped her chest. "He's in here and smiling down at me. It's okay, Lily."

"Contact Gage and the lawyer. You'll feel better after you've done that." I stood up. I wasn't trying to rush her out the door, but I needed to review my notes from the real estate transactions and get ready for customers.

As Jerilyn got to her feet, she said, "Thank you for talking to me. You're always coolheaded; I admire that. I wish I looked at things the way you did. I usually run off half-cocked and deal with the consequences later."

I wondered if she was referring to accepting Teddy's marriage proposal, considering their relationship remained a secret. Now to come out and announce they were to have been married would be uncomfortable for her. Jerilyn said goodbye, walked out, and closed the door behind her. Hopefully, Gage could help her and the lawyer, too.

"I thought she'd never leave." Milo got up and stretched.

"She's going to have a tough go with Teddy's family. I got the impression they, or at least his cousin, did not know Teddy and Jerilyn were seeing each other, let alone serious enough to get engaged."

"Doesn't it make you wonder why?" Milo wandered in my direction, pausing at my feet long enough for me to scratch his ears before moving to the counter. He strutted around like he owned the place more than I did.

"I've discovered Teddy was an odd duck."

Milo growled his lion imitation. "Don't go insulting the waterfowl population. What did they ever do to you?"

"Ha. All I meant was in all the years he went to movie night, he kept to himself. Only in the last few months did he get friendly with Marshall and Jill. I think that was because of the bribery issues going on. Camaraderie and all."

"I'm more interested in learning what you discovered about Pembroke Real Estate. You're holding out on me."

I pulled my notebook from the tote under the counter. Tapping the top, I said, "I might have struck gold."

He waved his paw over the cover. "I'm waiting."

I turned to the section where I madly scribbled notes. "Teddy Roberts was the busiest sales agent in the county. I believe I've only scratched the surface. But almost every building—residential or commercial—he sold went for under the listing price."

"That's normal. No one pays asking." Milo yawned as if he was already bored by my findings.

"No. Way under. Like below assessed value." I was warming up to my discovery. "If that was the case, how was he making money hand over fist? We see by the car he recently purchased and the rock he bought for Jerilyn that he wasn't hurting for cash."

"Loans. Credit cards. You've heard of those because you use them, and I know for a fact you have a car loan on your little white and blue Mini Cooper."

I gave him a sharp look.

"I can't help but overhear when every month you complain about writing the checks for the payments. And it's your job to keep me in kibble and catnip."

He had a point, and I let that drop. "Getting back to Teddy. What if...?" I thought about what I was going to say next. "What if he was doing dirty deals with buyers? Getting kickbacks from each sale, off the books."

"How?"

Now I had Milo's attention. "For example—and these are just fictional numbers—a house is on the market for one hundred thousand. The assessed value is $80K, but it sells for $75K, when what would have been more normal was a selling price of $90K. It's a cash deal and the owner is thrilled that the transaction is complete. But Teddy gets a cash bonus from the new buyer of $5K besides his commission, which effectively the seller pays him. Several percentage points of the deal and cash under the table and the new buyer still makes out. Everyone is happy until someone figures out what he's doing, confronts him, and things get out of hand."

"And they kill him? Sounds a little far-fetched. Are you going to run your theory by Gage?"

I closed my notebook, which had a list of sellers and their new addresses. "Not yet. I want to check out a few things. Talk to some of his previous clients and get a feel for their satisfaction with Teddy as a sales agent."

"Smart. When are you going to start?"

I glanced at my watch. "In about ten minutes. I'm headed over to the hardware store to chat up Tucker Gleason. He sold his house and moved into his parents' place out on Shore Road."

"How much do you think he was swindled out of?"

"Ballpark? Thirty thousand."

If a cat could whistle, the sound that came out of Milo's mouth would have been one. "That's a lot of reasons for revenge."

Five minutes later, my best friend Nikki walked into the bookshop. "Morning." She was wearing jeans, a black turtleneck with a deep-blue jacket, and black ballet flats. Her strawberry-blonde hair had been pulled back in a sleek ponytail and her eyes matched the jacket perfectly.

"Thanks for covering me. I need to run over to the hardware store and pick up"—I glanced around—"batteries."

With a wave of her hand, she laughed. "Yeah. Right. You're off sleuthing again." She quirked a brow. "Teddy's car accident?"

I leaned in. Not that I had any customers, but you just never knew in this town who could be ready to waltz in. "He was shot. The car accident was the added pizzazz to murder."

I filled her in with what I had learned at the town hall. She gave a low whistle. "Why, that little sneak. Who knew Teddy had it in him?"

"Nikki, I don't have facts yet. It's all supposition, but that's why I'm going to start with Tucker. His house was the most recent sale, and I want to gauge how he felt about it."

She walked behind the counter and tidied up with a grin. "Go. I'll handle the hordes of customers. But I will have a full report when you get back."

I walked into the hardware store. Conversation died. Nate was at the cash register, along with Tucker and a few other men I recognized.

"Morning." I moved down the aisle to where I knew the batteries were. I scanned the shelves, trying to come up with an obscure reason to talk to Tucker away from the group. I stepped into the main aisle. "Tucker, I can't seem to find triple-A batteries."

He stepped from behind the counter and hurried down the hall in my direction. As if on autopilot, he pulled a package from the shelf and handed it to me. He looked over his shoulder. "I'm glad you came in this morning. I'm in trouble, and I don't know what to do. I was going to come over to the bookstore later, but now that you're here, would you come into the back room with me so we can talk in private?" His words came out in a rush, and he took a ragged breath. "Please, Lily. I have no one else to turn to."

I nodded.

"Nate, I need to help Lily find a different battery. Will you keep an eye on things for me?"

I caught Nate's eye, and he tipped his head as if questioning what I wanted to do.

With a slight nod to him, Nate said, "Sure thing."

Tucker ushered me in ahead of him and the door closed ominously behind us, effectively shutting me off from everyone. I chewed the corner of my lower lip.

"I'm scared I'm going to be arrested."

I knew he was insinuating something about Teddy, but I could wait for him to spill the rest of what was on his mind.

"He screwed me over on the sale of my house, and two days ago, we had a huge argument at the Copper Kettle." He shook his head. "I said some things I shouldn't have."

"Like what exactly?" I knew what the next words would be to come from his mouth.

"If he didn't stop cheating people and make things right with my house sale, I was going to make sure that I was the last person he swindled."

Chapter 9
Gage

I walked into Lily's bookshop, expecting to see her chalkboard behind the counter with her making notes. I was surprised to see Nikki ringing up a customer, and by the looks, it was a happy tourist.

"And you say my husband and I should try the Clam Bake for dinner?" She tucked the paperback into an oversized tote bag with the word Maine in all capital letters on one side.

"Great seafood and plenty of it, and the desserts, if you have room, are also delicious. Even homemade by a local."

What Nikki didn't say is they were made by her, but I needed to interject. "The carrot cake is my favorite."

The woman turned and gave me a sunny smile. "Thank you so much. It is my favorite." She patted her midsection. "I'll need to do some more walking before we have dinner. We just stopped and had a bite at the Sweet Spot."

She smacked her lips, and I chuckled. "We have excellent restaurants in town. Enjoy your stay."

"It's been lovely so far; the town is charming." She smiled all the way out the door. Gage saw a man stand up from the bench and take the bag from her. "A safe bet, her husband."

"Cute couple." Nikki stuck the spike of the sale slip holder with the receipt. "How can I help you today?"

I looked around. "Where is the lovely Lily?"

"You know Lily. She's out and about." She gave me a thoughtful look. "When was the last time you talked to her?"

That wasn't what I wanted to hear. "Two days ago, when she stopped at the station and handed in her statement regarding her front window being smashed."

She held up her hand and smirked. "There's a been a murder, and you know Lily, and you haven't talked to her for two full days?" Shaking her head, she said, "You are so behind."

I could hear the semi tease and reproach in her tone. "In my defense, I've been busy." But my curiosity piqued. "What's been going on? Has Lily been checking into things?" I didn't need to say about Teddy's murder; it was implied. And the word investigation, in conjunction with Lily, gave me the shudders.

"You'll need to talk with her. I'm just the hired help at the moment."

Her smile did nothing to soothe my radar ping. "Where is she now?"

She thought for a minute. "At town hall again. It seems real estate transactions are very interesting." She gave me a wink. "You should swing by and see what might go on."

With a quick goodbye, I hurried out and down the street to Pembroke Town Hall. Taking the cement steps two at a time, I went inside. I knew where the registry of deeds was and moved down the hall, but I stopped when I glimpsed Lily in the tax collector's office.

She looked up and held up a finger. I waited for her in the hallway. It seemed like forever until she thanked the clerk and came out to meet me.

"Gage. I didn't expect to see you here. How about you buy me a cup of coffee?"

She tapped the cover on her notebook. If I had to guess, she had something interesting to share with me. I was going to have to fess up and let her know I had been running against a brick wall so far, and if Dax had learned anything, he wasn't sharing.

I pulled open the door and Lily walked out ahead of me. Coming up the steps was Ross Frederick. I hadn't seen him since the day of Teddy's death.

"Hey, Ross." I extended my hand, but he didn't shake it.

"Hello," he fumed. "That no good Teddy Roberts is still giving me trouble."

Lily and I stopped, and I asked, "Anything I can do to help?"

"Did you know I wanted to buy that empty storefront on Cove Avenue?"

How would I have known that? But I nodded anyway.

Seconds later, he sputtered, "The deal fell through and the reason why? Tucker said he would not let it go for the price we verbally agreed to. He said it was below assessed value and it was worth more. I had a lot riding on that deal." He stormed past us and into the building.

I looked at Lily, who seemed to be ready to burst at the seams. "Come on. We need to talk." She pulled on my arm, and I ran with her down the steps. She glanced at me. "Coffee and sweets in the park. Less chance of us being overheard."

There was an open park bench with no one close by. "I'll meet you there." Before she could answer, I jogged to the Sweet Shop and went inside. It was crazy busy. William was running the front counter, and a teenager was bussing small bistro tables.

"William." I waved from the side of the counter. There were people standing, three deep, waiting to place orders. "Okay if I grab two coffees and come back later to settle up?" He nodded and withdrew two muffins from the case and slid them into a paper sack and tossed the bag to me. I gave him another wave and filled two cups with coffee. Nothing fancy today.

When I got back to the town square, Lily had moved to a different bench closer to her shop. Not that the park was huge, but people were clustering around where we had been. She stood up and took the bag once I was almost at the table.

"The Sweet Spot was rockin', so William put some muffins in the bag. I'm not sure about the flavor."

She took the cup. "Thank you." When she sat down, I hadn't even taken a sip of coffee before she said in a low and controlled voice, "Teddy is lucky. Based on what I found, he's been behaving badly for quite some time. He's made many people furious and more will be, once they all find out."

"What was he doing?" I knew he wasn't the most like-able guy. He was a caricature of a sleazy car salesperson, but he sold real estate.

"I don't know who is behind the deal, but he was encouraging people to take less for their homes and busi-nesses and got cash kickbacks. Whoever killed Teddy was out for revenge."

"Sounds like Teddy had two reasons for his death. Money and possibly revenge."

Lily pulled a cranberry muffin from the bag and handed it to me. I broke it in half and set it aside.

"I'm convinced it was a business deal gone wrong." She didn't start eating her muffin but looked in the direction of the hardware store. "I saw Tucker. He's concerned he'll be arrested for Teddy's murder, but he was small potatoes compared to a few other transactions."

"Tell me what you found, and I'll be the judge." I leaned back in the chair to pull out my notebook from my pants pocket.

She waited until I opened it to a blank page. "Teddy was bringing in a ton of money. People thought it was from commission and it was in a way, but someone was buying up chunks of real estate. A group called Davis Corporation. Teddy was their only real estate agent. From what I can find, for the last year, he's been selling homes under the assessed value, and based on a ledger I saw, he was receiving cash kickbacks. Not in the same amount as the difference between the sales prices and tax assessments but significant, and the new owner is still saving thousands by doing the deals this way."

I jotted down a few notes. "Do you think this was why he was paying Flora off? She found out what he was doing?"

Lily nodded. "I do. And I think when he first started dating Jerilyn, it was to get access to her parents' home. I think that was the first time he got a special reward."

"If it all started with the Busch house, that was prime real estate. Oceanfront, with unlimited business potential for a luxury hotel."

She tapped the tabletop with her nail. "And it went for almost two hundred thousand less than the assessed value when it should have gone for at least four hundred thousand over assessed. When I spoke to Gretchen Wilson, from

Wilson Realty and Teddy's competition, she said he schmoozed potential clients. Told them he could sell their house fast, with a cash deal for a quick close."

"Dangling a fast sale and cash would be enough to lure plenty of clients his way. Add to that he was the local guy and Gretchen was a newcomer to the area."

"I'd hardly call ten years new." She nodded in the direction of the hardware store. "Don't look now, but here comes Tucker."

I didn't look up. I just waited until he stopped next to us. "Morning, Tucker." I sipped my coffee, wanting to appear casual.

"Gage. Lily. Sorry for the interruption, but I was hoping we could talk. If you have the time to spare."

"Just having coffee and a little conversation." As if to prove my point, I popped a piece of the muffin into my mouth. It was darn good.

Tucker shifted his weight from one foot to the other. "I'm sure Lily told you I was plenty upset with Teddy. But I want you to hear it from me. I didn't kill him. I know he died in a car accident, but I didn't even wish for him to kick the bucket. Just to get what was coming to him." His face flushed. "Not that he deserved to die, you understand. More like a comeuppance with the law. He was dirty dealing. And yes, I was one of the people he screwed over with the sale of my house, but I didn't do anything like rig his car to hit the pole."

The fact that Tucker had yet to mention a gunshot was good news. It hadn't hit the gossip train. That was only a matter of time. I continued to eat my muffin to see what else he might say and thankfully Lily was learning how to wait out a person too.

"Gage, you gotta believe me." He wrung his hands and

the pleading tone in his voice was my cue to let this poor man off the hook. For now.

"Tucker, I appreciate you coming out here to talk to me. We have a few people that we're interested in talking to. You are one of them since you may have been a victim of his."

Before I could go any further, he interrupted. "Not might have been. I was. The man he sold my house to bought it for way under the value. Gretchen Wilson warned me, but I didn't listen. Teddy told me she was chewing on sour grapes, and I shouldn't listen to her."

That was an interesting tidbit that Gretchen had approached Tucker before he signed with Teddy. "How long before you signed the sales agreement with Teddy did you speak with Gretchen?"

"I'm not sure. Two, maybe three days." He jammed his hands in his pants pockets. "Now that you mention it, I'm not even sure how she found out. I never contacted her."

"It's a small town, and I'm sure real estate people talk to each other. I wouldn't give that another thought." I gave him a curt nod. "I appreciate you coming over to talk with me, and I may need you to come into the station for a formal statement."

"I understand. I just wanted you to hear the truth from me." He gave Lily a weak smile. "When I talked to Lily, she encouraged me to call you, but it's hard, you know. Thinking that the person you need to talk to might consider you a suspect and, heck, maybe even arrest you." He shuddered as if the temperature suddenly dropped thirty degrees.

"It's fine, but next time call me directly. Lily is a good listener, but as a detective, we can speed up the process of what happened from your point of view if you talk to the officials."

"Got it." He jabbed his finger in the direction of his store. "I need to get back. I left Ross minding the register." He lifted his hand. "Thanks again, Gage. See you around, Lily."

The man looked as if someone had lifted a heavy weight from his shoulders as he made his way back across the square.

I looked at Lily. "Anyone else you've spoken to over the last couple of days?"

With a cheeky grin, she said, "Of course. And I'm ready to share my observations." She took the last crumb of my muffin. "As long as you don't tell me to stop helping."

"You know that's my go-to response every time you want to put your sleuth hat on." My heart constricted just thinking about Lily out there asking questions to people she thought were her neighbors when it was obvious one of them had murder on their minds. And if she asked the right question to the wrong person, she could become the next victim. I'd have to solve the crime before she walked into something that might get her hurt or, worse, killed.

She leaned forward. "What Tucker just said was very interesting. Gretchen never mentioned that she knew Teddy was being underhanded before the deals happened." Drumming her fingers on the picnic table, she pursed her lips while her brain whirled. "Is it possible that it did not thrill her that Teddy was snapping up all the prime sales and then to discover he was doing dirty deals? Not just harming the locals, but who was he helping buy up property and why?"

"I'd hazard a guess that might lead up to who killed him."

Lily's eyes grew wide. "Do you think he reconsidered his business ethics and whoever was behind all the purchases got mad and took him out of the equation so he wouldn't squeal?"

I truly loved the way she described things. Squealing made me think of a pig, which the way I was looking at Teddy now was kind.

Lily clasped my arm with a death grip. "Don't look now —well, you need to. Gretchen and Jerilyn are near the pole. And it is not a heartfelt exchange of condolences."

Chapter 10
Lily

I was on my feet and running toward the two women with Gage on my heels. Jerilyn had pulled back her hand as if she was about to slap Gretchen.

"*Stop!*" My voice cracked the air, and Jerilyn's eyes grew wide as she looked at me. A flash of relief washed over Gretchen's.

"What is going on here?" I really needed to think about working out as I drew in deep, ragged breaths.

Gretchen took two steps back from Jerilyn. "She was accusing me of killing Teddy. Demanding to know if I owned a gun. And if that is the way I intended to grow my business, by getting rid of the competition."

Red in the face, Jerilyn said, "Teddy told me how you confronted him about all the sales he was making. He said if you couldn't handle it, then maybe you needed to find a new line of work or move someplace where no one knew your reputation as a terrible real estate agent."

Gretchen's lips thinned. "You are under misguided or lovestruck notions. He wasn't superior to me in any way. If you knew the things he had done, you wouldn't be so—"

The next words died on her lips, and she shook her head. "I need to get back to my office."

Gage said, "I trust you ladies will keep clear of each other?"

They glared at each other, but neither spoke up and said they would or wouldn't.

"Ladies. I would hate to arrest you for assault, so avoid each other at all costs."

Nodding their heads, Gretchen moved toward her sedan which was parked on the opposite side of the green. Jerilyn glared as the other woman walked away without a backward glance. "How dare she insinuate Teddy was anything less than an honest businessman? She didn't like it because people were giving him the contracts over her and he found highly motivated buyers."

Either she was clueless, or she didn't care that her fiancé was a snake. "Jerilyn, not everyone is going to be everyone else's biggest fan, and if Gretchen and Teddy were in the middle of a little rivalry, it's understandable she isn't heartbroken that her competition is gone."

She whirled on her heel and glared at me. "He's not just gone like on vacation or something. He's dead. She killed him."

Gage asked, "Do you have proof?" His voice was calm, and she sneered at him. It was obvious her grief had overwhelmed her today.

"It all comes down to money. He was making it and driving her business under. Isn't that the oldest reason in the book for murder?" Her gaze shifted to me. "How would you like it if another bookstore was in town and taking all of your sales? You'd be angry."

How dare she turn this around on me. It's not like I was instrumental in his death. It was a good thing I hadn't learned more magic. If I had, there was no telling if I wouldn't have hurled a spell to spice up this conversation. "Not enough to take another's life. You need to be cautious, throwing around accusations."

"You're such a Goody Two-shoes." She looked at Gretchen's receding car taillights. "Maybe I should be careful. Who knows, I might be next on her hit list." She stalked off in the opposite direction, and I couldn't help but notice she wasn't going to the Sweet Shop.

"Gage, shouldn't Jerilyn be at work?"

With a shrug, he said, "I don't think she's been to the bakery since the day of the accident." He looked at his watch. "I need to get down to the police station, but I'd like to finish our conversation later. Is it okay if I swing by the store this afternoon?"

I nodded and watched Jerilyn continue to walk down the block. Where was her car? "Swing by anytime. I'm headed back now."

"Don't worry about what she said. Being a nice person suits you perfectly." He gestured to the table. "Would you mind tossing my cup?"

"Sure. And it's fine. I've been called worse, I'm sure." Gage walked away, and I gathered the remains of our coffee and muffins. I had work to do and maybe even this afternoon I'd be able to perfect a new spell. As Milo reminded me daily, I was woefully behind on my training, and all I needed to do was read the book.

I slammed the big book of *Practical Beginnings* shut and groaned. "I'm never going to master the levitation spell."

Milo was stretched across the counter. "Not with that attitude, you won't." He waved his paw over the book again and it flipped open to the page I was just on. "Making an object float is one of the easiest spells. For some reason, you think you actually need to hold the object up. But you don't. With levitation, everything is weightless. It's your mind that does the heavy lifting." He made a strange, almost satisfied meow. He placed his paw on a pen. "You're going to levitate this pen. Now pick it up. Look at it. Feel it. Turn it over in your hand. Tell me everything you notice about it."

I did as he instructed. "The barrel is smooth. Cool to the touch." I placed it in the palm of my hand. "It doesn't weigh much."

"Close your eyes and repeat after me. In relaxation, there is levitation. The, insert object name, is weightless and chainless and now can hover until I uncover. This is my wish, so shall it be."

I moved to put the pen back on the counter when a kitty growl emanated from Milo.

"Leave it in your hand."

I centered it and closed my eyes. The, insert object name, is—"

Milo interrupted me. "Pen. The pen is weightless. Now concentrate just on the pen and the sound of my voice. You can feel the cool, smooth pen, the featherlight weight of it lingering on your palm. Now, in your mind, picture a space between your skin and the cool, smooth barrel."

I wanted to giggle as I said verbatim what he'd asked, then I concentrated on what it felt like to have air between the object and my hand. I squeezed my eyes tighter and forced my thoughts to focus completely on the air surrounding the pen.

Milo was making encouraging remarks. "Concentrate. Focus. Focus."

I'm not sure if it was wishing, but I felt air on my skin. I cracked open one eye. The pen was hovering above my hand by at least two inches.

"Focus, Lily. Keep it steady."

I opened the other eye as I continued concentrating on that pen. Everything else fell away. The surrounding room was irrelevant. The pen moved higher. I wanted it to dance. The pen turned end over end. I was doing it. The bell on the door chimed. I lost my focus, and it fell to the floor.

Gage was hovering in the open doorway, his face scrunched up, looking puzzled. "Did I just see a pen in midair?"

Darn it. How will I get out of this one? "You did."

Milo hissed. "What are you doing?"

I waved my hand and the big book closed, but Gage had bent down to get the pen. "I'm trying to learn some magic tricks. You know me and puzzles." I gave him what I hoped was a convincing smile. "I have to solve them." I hoped my explanation sounded plausible, but inside I was jumping up and down. What was going to be the next thing I could work on and does the spell work if the object isn't in my hand?

He handed me the pen. "You'll need to show me how to do it after you perfect it."

Milo got up from the counter. "Yeah, right. Mortal." He hopped down and padded out of the room. He paused in the doorway. "I'm going out. Meet you at home."

Choosing to ignore him, I turned back to Gage. "I didn't expect to see you."

He narrowed his eyes. "We talked about it after you broke up the ladies' argument."

I nodded. "Oh. Right." I needed to avoid him circling back to the pen floating in midair. "It's been busy in here today." I crossed my fingers behind my back, knowing that he would think I was referring to book sales. I'd let him. In reality, I was busy doing witchy things.

"Do you have time to finish our conversation?" From behind his back, he pulled out an iced coffee. "Bribe?"

I laughed. "It's nice that you thought of me, but you never need to resort to bribery." I tipped my head. "Well, maybe almost never."

He chuckled. "I'll keep that in mind."

I dragged my chalkboard out from behind the counter. "We have three people to discuss. Tucker, Gretchen, and Jerilyn." I jammed the straw in my coffee and took a long sip. Darn, that hit the spot. I could feel the caffeine jolt jump-starting my brain. "The outburst we witnessed this morning was a heartbroken woman who lost her fiancé. Her dreams were crushed, and she was lashing out, which is completely understandable." I wrote their names down with a dash after each one.

Gage nodded. "I agree. I wish there was something more we could do to help her."

"Even sadder, his cousin is cutting her out of making final arrangements. I suggested she contact a lawyer to see what her options are, being his fiancée and all."

"That's a good idea. Hopefully, that will give her some peace," he said. "Can we sit?" Grabbing the easel, he set it in front of our usual chairs. "Let's talk about Tucker."

"Well." I chewed the end of the pen that I'd just been levitating. "He's anxious that he'll be named a suspect, and since he came to us, I'm inclined to think he's innocent."

"On the other hand, he could be a master at deflecting. Oversharing all those details could be a skilled attempt to look completely transparent when in reality he's the guilty party."

"Okay, so he might have a motive." I wrote *money* next

to his name. "We need to go back to the basics." On the board, I wrote: *Gunshot* with an arrow pointing to the words *car accident.* "If he was already dead, considering there was no bullet hole in the windshield, how did he have the accident?"

He gave me a congratulatory smile. "I wondered how long it would take for you to ask that question." He rubbed his hands together with glee. "Whoever it was shot him in the right temple. The passenger window shattered. Per the coroner's preliminary report, if the gunshot hadn't killed him instantly, the combo of the shooting and head-on collision would have, since he wasn't wearing a seat belt."

"So that means..."

Gage was bobbing his head and grinning. "Go on."

"He was shot from the same side of the street as the hardware store."

He slapped the arm of the wingback chair. "Exactly!"

Something was wrong with that. "Bee Bee's Boutique is right next to Tucker's place. Which means Beatrice should be back on the suspect list."

"I've ruled out William since the Sweet Spot had customers spilling out on the sidewalk when I arrived."

"And Gretchen could have been in any of the stores and easily pulled the trigger. But do they all own guns? I think the shells found were from a nine millimeter." Next to Gretchen, I wrote *money* again.

He gave me a sharp look. "How did you know that? We haven't talked about it."

I gave him my best innocent look. "You must have told me. Otherwise, I couldn't have possibly known."

Suspicion clouded his eyes. "You haven't learned how to hack computers, have you?"

Now I pretended to be shocked. "I might be overly

curious at times, but I would never, under any circumstances, knowingly break the law."

He held up his hands in defense. "I'm sorry. Sometimes you worry me with your overzealous nature. I wanted to put it out there."

"It was out, and now, put it back in." There was a part of me that was actually bruised that Gage would say something like that.

"I'm sorry, Lily. This whole thing has me on edge. I know you've been asking questions, trying to help, and it scares me. The last time—"

I jumped on that statement since I knew where it was going. "That won't happen again. Besides, I'm looking at public records, and people are coming to me to talk. I haven't had to try to get someone to slip up and talk to me."

He looked satisfied with my explanation. I wasn't about to mention that if I needed to branch out and seek answers, I would. In my mind, that went without actually verbalizing it.

"So that leaves Gretchen. We know her business has been suffering for the last year. Teddy had been snapping up all the prime contracts with the best chance for commission. I found out how many houses she sold last year and, a rough estimate if she made the full percentage, she was under six figures."

"Any idea how that compares to the previous couple of years?"

Now I had captured his full attention. "In the last three years, she grossed well over six figures. That makes quite a decent amount in a bank account."

"Not to mention her ego." Gage got up and paced the length of the room. "I need to take a harder look at her."

The doorknob rattled, causing me to look up. Dax was

on the other side, trying to come in. It was as if the door was locked.

Gage crossed and pulled the door open. "Dax. I didn't expect to see you here."

The lawman looked from me to Gage and back to me. "I wanted to speak with Lily to see if she had any new theories."

I thought of the easel and wished I had learned an erasing spell. That was going to be next on my list. Instead, I thought about Milo swishing his tail across the chalkboard just enough to smear the writing. In my mind, I could see it happening. Under my breath, I said, "I wish it be."

My familiar didn't appear as I had hoped, and Dax was coming closer. It would be mere seconds before he saw the names and ideas next to them.

"What are you working on?" He noted the iced coffee cups and the easel.

I could feel my heart rate increase. How could I explain that Gage was discussing the case with me? Even if Dax knew it to be a possibility, there was no sense throwing my best friend under Dax's black sedan. "Oh, not much, just catching up." I glanced at the easel and did a double take. It was blank.

Chapter 11
Lily

A sigh of relief escaped my lungs. I couldn't explain it, but I must have cast a spell that made a little magic. With a mental note to ask Milo later, I flashed Gage a crooked smile. He probably thought I had erased it, and I wasn't about to explain. "See, nothing on here to talk about. The children's story hour is next Saturday, and I need to add a reminder." I really hated that I had to use another harmless fib, but I wasn't about to admit the truth. I still didn't have confidence that Dax was on the right side of the law. There was no sense in tipping him off to anything.

Dax cocked a brow as if he didn't believe me, but heck, I wouldn't either if I were in his shoes. After all, I had a track record of getting involved in things that were police business.

"Do you have a few minutes to talk?" He looked at Gage and back at me. "Unless, of course, I am interrupting?"

Avoidance was key. "I always have time to talk to you," I said. "Would you like a coffee or a glass of water?"

"No. Thank you." He tried to give me a smile, but it wasn't something that seemed to come easily to him. "I understand there was a dustup earlier today across the street between two ladies."

How had he heard about that? Was there a mole in town? I thought of who was trying their best to stay off the radar. Tucker. Which the more he seemed to profess his innocence, the louder it screamed that he seemed guilty.

"Nothing major. Jerilyn is obviously upset that her fiancé died, and Gretchen and Teddy were business competitors. I think it's natural for emotions to run high." I hoped I had downplayed it enough, but the way his dark, almost black, eyes widened, I knew something had struck a nerve in what I had said.

"There's no evidence Teddy was engaged to anyone."

"It happened the night before the accident. There wasn't any time for an announcement."

His eyes widened again as if to say, really? What did Dax know that I didn't? I glanced at Gage. Did he know what Dax was alluding to? "Have you learned nothing that might be useful?"

I didn't appreciate his probing manner. "Everything I've learned is public record." I felt the frown slip over my lips. "Teddy was not the stand-up businessman I had thought. He was into shady dealings and cheating people, and its obvious someone was tired of his shenanigans."

"You feel it's someone local who killed him?"

Dax gave me a penetrating gaze, as if he were grilling me under lights at the police station. Whatever branch of law enforcement he was in, I bet he had suspects folding under the pressure on a regular basis.

"I don't know who killed him. I believe we can tie it back to money. As the saying goes, it's the root of all evil."

With a one-shoulder shrug, he said, "If you learn something of interest, you'll contact me?"

The question didn't hang in the air. I was nodding before he even finished speaking. It was never a good idea to upset a potential adversary. "Absolutely."

If he believed me, it was hard to be sure. He gave me a curt nod. "Take care, Lily."

Why did every person remind me to be careful? I wasn't a child, and I had skills more than likely they didn't. Plus, I had Milo.

"You too, Dax." I escorted him to the door and Gage pulled it open. Dax left without another word. I closed the door firmly and whirled around. "He was on a fishing expedition."

"But you weren't biting. Why didn't you tell him what you had learned at the town hall? As you said, it's a matter of public record." I went back to get my iced coffee and glanced at the easel.

"And how did you get that cleaned off before Dax saw it?"

I gave him a wide smile. "Magic." This time, it wasn't a fib. Since I didn't know for sure until I talked with Milo, it was the only answer I could give.

He winked. "Keep that up, and we can hire you out for parties."

There was no way I'd be doing that, but Gage could think it. "Dax said something interesting, and I think you caught it. Why was he hung up on the recent engagement?"

"Maybe he's against marriage? Or he couldn't picture the two of them together. I'm not sure, but I've been thinking about Dax and why he's in town and taking charge of this case." Gage picked up the easel and put it behind the counter, out of the way. He then took a long drink of his coffee.

I wished he'd stop stalling; it was driving me nuts. "What Teddy was supposedly doing was illegal but hardly worthy of a federal officer's time."

"That's where you're wrong. White-collar crime, like fraud in a real estate transaction, is a federal crime that would come with hefty fines and jail time. I need to find out who's behind the purchases. What do they plan to do with the real estate? Flip the properties and make more money, which Teddy could have helped them with too."

"Hold on. I just had a thought." I walked to the display of town, county, and state maps for sale on a twirl rack. I pulled out the town map and spread it on the counter. Next, I got a highlighter and Post-it notes. Then I withdrew my notebook from my bag.

"Lily, what are you thinking?"

"If we map all the sales Teddy handled in the last twelve months, it may give us a pattern as to what was sold. Are they random homes with potential new businesses coming to town? There has to be logic behind all of this." I waved my hands over the illustrated tourist map. It wasn't to scale, but it was a great visual.

I plotted the most recent sales and worked my way back to the first one, which I suspected was Jerilyn's parents' oceanfront home. There had to be over twenty properties, and some were worth a lot of money if we looked at the assessed values.

Then I put the actual sales cost down and the amount of the typical commission. I tapped the commission figure. "This would have given him a decent life, but not enough to buy expensive diamond rings and fancy cars, and remember last month he was talking about going on a very special vacation."

"I do. You thought he and Jill were running off together and crushing Marshall Stone's heart?"

I jabbed a highlighter close to his chest. "Marshall is in love with Jill. She just needs to open her eyes and see the wonderful man standing in front of her."

Gage's Adam's apple bobbed. "Seems there's a lot of that going on."

That was a confusing statement. Everyone I knew was happily paired up. "We're not responsible for getting those two to open their eyes."

His shoulders appeared to droop. "I'm going to see what I can find out about whoever bought the properties. Our answer will lie there."

"I'll make you a copy of this, so you don't need to duplicate work." He waited but didn't say anything more, and I wasn't sure what I might have said to upset him. He was an adult. If I had, he needed to speak up.

After he glanced at the copy and said thanks, he started for the door. "Gage. Dinner tonight. My place?"

"Not tonight, Lily. But thanks anyway."

After he left, I slumped against the counter. Milo hopped up. "Detective Cutie didn't want to come for dinner at your place? I wonder if he's sick."

With a quick glance at Milo, I said, "Why would you think that?"

"The man never turns down dinner with you. Maybe he's got a hot date."

That stopped my heart. Gage dating. "Do you know something or just trying to wind me up?"

"Lily. I always have your best interests at heart, but

witch, when are you going to tell him you think he's the best part of dinner? A man likes to hear those kinds of things."

Before I could respond, he tapped the cover of the big book of spells. "Tell me, how did you wipe the easel clear? It was genius on your part." He gave me a side-eye. "We haven't worked on disappearing spells, or have you been reading at night?"

I shook my head. "No to the reading, and I'm not sure how it happened. One minute I was calling to you in my head and Dax was walking in my direction. I thought about your tail swishing over the chalkboard and I breathed, then said, *I wish it be*. When I looked down, it was clean."

Stretching one of his back legs out in front of him, Milo tugged the fur between his toes with his teeth. "That's an interesting development," he said between pulls. "Your book might work with you." He continued to work on the other foot.

"What do you mean by that?"

He gave me an annoyed look as if I had interrupted him meditating or something else equally important. "My dear witch. You have a lot of catching up to do in your education of spells and other witchy delights."

"Such as flying?" My heart soared like my body wanted to.

He shook his head. "Give up the flying stuff. I've told you before that is in the way distant future, if ever. Witches actually flying is very rare." He arched his back, and I stroked his soft gray head.

"I know what you're going to say next. Read the book." I dropped a kiss on his nose, and he didn't grumble, so I knew he was soaking up the attention. "But somehow, I cleaned the board without knowing what I was doing. Flying might not be far off."

"Talk to Mimi and see what she says, or Nikki, for that matter. After all, she's a kitchen witch. If anyone can fly a broom, it would be her." He hopped off the counter, but before he stalked away, he turned and looked at me. "Oh, and for the record. Gretchen was in the green the whole time leading up to and right after Teddy's accident." He trotted from the room after he dropped that tidbit.

What was my next step? I was itching to close the shop, but it was only three. I needed more information about Teddy and Jerilyn. Who would have the inside scoop.? She didn't have any real friends in town. She had always been a loner. It was understandable since she'd never moved out of her parents' house until it had been sold. Now she was living... I stopped. Where was Jerilyn living?

"Milo?" I wandered down the aisle of books that were his favorite place to snooze. Sure enough, he was curled up on the pillow I placed in between the bookshelf and the window seat. He could look outside if he was so inclined.

"I'm napping." His little lion growl didn't faze me.

"Any idea where Jerilyn is living?"

"What do I look like to you? A real estate agent or the phone book?" He yawned. "Ask William. He must know since she works at his bakery."

The second point was good; the first was just impertinent. "The bakery closes at two. I'll have to stop in before I open tomorrow." Milo had shut his eyes again. Our conversation was over.

I had questions, and in order to clear my head, I needed to write them down. The bell on the door jingled. Time to take care of my customers.

After the high school kids left with CliffsNotes for *Macbeth*, I withdrew my notebook from my tote where I had stashed it after Gage left.

Jerilyn Busch - home?
Jill and Marshall - Teddy's friends- what do they know
Gretchen - location at time of shooting/accident
Tucker - why so nervous?
Everyone - nine mil gun?

I ran down my lists. I had a lot of questions, and the only way to get answers was to talk to people. Research had given me some facts. Once I knew what Marshall and Jill knew about Teddy's romantic life, that would solve one question. But how would I find out information about Gretchen without asking her directly, and what did I need to know? I needed a nonjudgmental sounding board. Nikki.

An hour later, I was sitting at Nikki's kitchen table with a mug of tea and a plate of butterscotch blondies sitting in front of me. She was mixing up cake batter for a birthday cake.

"How many cake orders do you have for this weekend?" I nibbled on the edge of the sweet buttery treat.

She brushed back a stray lock of blonde hair from her face. "I have a wedding cake for one hundred and fifty people, this birthday cake, and mini cupcakes for Gretchen."

I perked up. "Gretchen? Is she having a party?"

"No. She likes to have mini cupcakes at her more important open houses. She's got one of the B and B's off Main Street. I think it's the Graham place. Usually she picks them up, so I'm not sure."

"Did Teddy ever do the same thing? Have refreshments at any of his open houses?"

"If he did, I never baked for him. But who knows? He was cheap, so he might have gotten slice and bake cookies from the market."

I couldn't help but laugh when she sneered as she said the words *slice and bake* and *market* in the same sentence. Nikki was talented in the kitchen, in part because she was a witch with a special gift, but she had been a great baker even when we were in school together.

"If I ever hold an open house at the bookstore, I promise to ask you to make the goodies."

She gave me that side-eye look that might have made others nervous, but I laughed. "You'd better or our friendship would be over. Or worse, I'd hex you."

My stomach dropped when I thought of putting a hex on someone. I remembered when I had done a spell without even knowing how. "I can do that, hex a person?"

She must have realized I was borderline horrified. "Relax. You're a white witch, not black. We can't do harm."

"Are you sure?" I heard the tremble in my voice and wished that a new seed of worry hadn't been planted.

"Relax. It's fine." She pushed the plate a little closer and said, "Finish your tea and cookie, and tell me what's on your mind. And when do we have to leave?"

"You're going to offer to deliver Gretchen's order to the open house."

"Seriously?"

"Yes." I gave her my best wide-eyed innocent look. "We're going house hunting."

She shook her head. "I can only imagine what we might find."

"I'm hoping for some answers to my growing list of questions." I hadn't bothered to pull out my notebook and show her. Tomorrow after I talked to William, I was going to make time to bump into Jill and hopefully Marshall too.

Chapter 12
Gage

The next morning, I saw Lily hurrying across the square from her shop. She was moving toward the Sweet Spot. I whistled, and she looked around before her face split into a wide grin and she changed directions and walked to where I was standing. My breath caught in my chest as she drew close. Her soft brown eyes sparkled, and I knew that look. She was up to something, and it was only a matter of time until I'd find out what.

"Gage. I didn't expect to see you out here this morning."

"Doing a little walk around."

She nodded. "Checking the scene again?"

Before I could answer, she said, "I've done that several times. Replaying what I saw last week and I'm still coming up empty. I know he died from the gunshot, but I never heard it. All I heard was the crash." She shuddered, as I'm sure she recalled that sound.

"Whoever fired the shot used a silencer."

She recoiled for a fraction of a second and then leaned into me. "Do you know what I discovered last night?"

"I do not know." She was so cute when she got that bookish grin.

"That you can also call a silencer a suppressor. They're actually used interchangeably. I was looking up information about the shell casings, and when I read it at first, I thought it was a misprint."

"That's true, but most folks use silencer."

She nodded. "I read that too, but are you sure? Bea said she heard something like a gun shot."

"She must have been something else." I nodded, reluctant to share all the details since I didn't want her to take the information and run with it. As she followed the trail of clues, I was positive she had uncovered more than I knew. "We're sure."

"What about the shell casings? If the perp"—she grinned as she used police jargon—"was careful enough to use the suppressor"—she winked—"why leave the casings behind?"

I looked around. Was anyone close enough to hear our conversation? I lowered my voice anyway. One never knew how conversations might carry. "The caliber that killed Teddy was a .22, not a nine millimeter."

"A ruse to distract." She nodded, her brow furrowed. "I'm assuming you've checked to see who has one registered."

Lily had a sharp brain, and if she had wanted to be a cop, she would have been amazing. "No one in our suspect pool." I nodded in the direction of Tucker's Hardware and then down the street toward Gretchen's office. "Tucker and Gretchen both have a powerful motive."

"Not just them. Everyone who used Teddy as a real estate agent for the last year might carry a grudge. When I was checking records, I realized you are right, and this potential scheme had to have started around the time he sold the Busch home."

"Do you think Jerilyn was unhappy with the transaction?" I knew Lily and Jerilyn had talked on a couple of occasions. Maybe she had let something slip.

Chewing her lower lip, she shook her head. "No. You won't swindle your girlfriend's family." A sharp look came into her eye. "I need to cross-reference who has remained in town after they sold their homes and see if I can remember where everyone was standing when I came out of my shop. No one was running in the car's direction. It was as if their feet were stuck in the cement." She tapped the center of her forehead. "I just need to remember."

"I'll see if Peabody and Mac have the locations where people were when they talked to onlookers. That might help too." Being focused on the investigation, I realized I had stopped Lily from her mission. "Where were you headed in such a hurry? Wanting to enjoy a muffin?"

"I was going to the bakery to talk to William. But I was looking for Jerilyn's address. I wanted to—" The pause gave it away. She was fishing. "Send her a condolence card," she said with a triumphant grin.

I was sure Lily would send a card now, but that wasn't the real reason behind the inquisition. "I'll ask Peabody to check." I withdrew my phone and called her.

"Good morning. I have you on speakerphone, and I'm with Lily."

She said, "Hi, Sharon."

After everyone exchanged pleasantries, I said, "Can you do me a quick favor and pull up Jerilyn Busch's address, please?"

"Sure, give me a minute."

The sound of keys clicking softly filled the moments.

Lily shifted from one foot to the other. How would I get her to tell me what she was up to next?

"Her address on file is Ten Ocean View Lane. But isn't that her parents' place?"

A satisfied look came over Lily's face. "She must not have updated the DMV yet. Thanks for checking, Peabody. See you later."

Lily chimed in again and said goodbye, and I disconnected the call. "Now, what do you intend to do with this information?"

She pointed to the bakery. "Ask William, of course. Like you said, she probably hasn't updated her driver's license yet. But I still would like to send a sympathy card."

"I'll walk you over and you can buy me a coffee today." We both strolled casually, but I could feel the tension emanating from Lily. "Penny for your thoughts?"

She smiled at the old-fashioned phrase, and it accomplished my goal, bringing her out of her headful of whirling ideas. "I wanted to visit with Jerilyn to see what she could tell me about the relationship, or lack of one, between Teddy and Gretchen. If she was jealous or upset with what was happening, would she have wanted to get him in trouble? And would she have taken matters into her own hands, placing a call to the FBI or whoever to get him into trouble? It was clear from the argument we witnessed yesterday, there is no love lost between the two women."

"True. But I can't picture Gretchen being vengeful, and Jerilyn is grieving. I'm sure she's just upset, and rightly so, that her fiancé is dead, and finally her happily ever after was within her reach."

"I agree. That is some of it." Lily's steps slowed as they drew closer to the bakery. "But she might know something that Teddy had said about Gretchen, which could help us close the case."

I took her hand and stopped her before she could cross the road. "Lily. We're not going to close this case. I will. Please do not—and I can't stress that enough—do not do anything to put yourself in harm's way."

"Don't worry. I'll be perfectly fine." She brushed her lips across my cheek, and the scent of her shampoo teased my senses. It was the same herbal blend she'd used since high school.

Taking a step back, she said, "I appreciate your concern. Thank you."

There it was. Her polite *mind your own business* tone. "I will worry about you. I always do."

She tipped her head and gave me a questioning look, but she didn't voice the thought she had. The door to the bakery opened and several people came out. I moved forward and grabbed the door to hold it for her. "After you."

She laughed. "I know. Coffee's on me."

I held up a hand to William and pointed to the to-go cups. I'd fix our coffee while Lily talked to William. One eye was on the door and the other on her. I wanted to see his face when she asked. Would he give Lily the address?

"Hi, William." She peered into the case.

He looked through the glass and gave her a wide, welcoming smile. "If it isn't my favorite bookseller. Any chance that new thriller about the archeologist is in yet?"

She nodded and smiled. "It is, and I put a copy aside for you, so no rush to get over. It's not going anywhere."

"Jeez, Lily, you're such a nice girl."

Gage couldn't agree with him more, and the faint color

that rose in her cheeks showed she appreciated the compliment.

"Thank you." She pointed to the muffins under a glass dome. "May I have two of those?"

"Good choice. You can never go wrong with a banana chocolate chip muffin." He slipped two into a white bag. "Anything else?"

She said, "I've got coffee too. It's my turn to pay today."

William looked over her shoulder at me and gave me a stern look. "In my day, the lady never paid."

Her cheeks flushed a deeper shade of pink. "It's fine. We like to take turns." Lily glanced at me and winked. "William, by any chance would you have Jerilyn's address? I'd like to send her a card."

"Ah, jeez, no, I don't. My bookkeeper takes care of all the paperwork. But you know I should send her a card too. When I find out, I'll let you know."

"Is she coming back to work soon?"

And there it was. The real reason Lily was curious. She had something on her mind.

"I sure hope so. But I told her to take all the time she needed. Losing Teddy like that after she finally finds the right guy for her." He shook his head. "Darn shame. But the heart heals."

He tapped his chest, and even from where I stood, I could see the tears fill his eyes. He was thinking about his late wife, Lulu. They had been each other's shadows. You never saw one without the other close by.

She reached across the counter and placed her hands over his. The sweet gesture came from Lily's heart.

The older man lifted his eyes and gave her a sad smile. "Don't spend your life waiting. Listen to your heart."

His gaze drifted to where I was standing. William knew

I was in love with Lily. His words stopped my heart. What if something happened to Lily, and she never knew how I felt about her? Could I live with that?

She gave his hands another squeeze. "I know you miss Lulu, but please remember you have many friends in this town, and we all loved her too."

"Thank you." He withdrew his hands from hers and passed her the bag. She handed him a few bills, and he waved her off. "Today's treats are on me."

She slipped around the end of the counter and wrapped her arms around the older man. And he smiled as she said something too soft for me to hear. Whatever it was caused him to laugh a little, too. "See you later, William."

"Goodbye, you two." He lifted his hand and turned to the next customer in line. He gave them the same amount of attention he had given Lily. That was his way. Everyone was important, just as it should be.

I pushed open the door and waited for Lily to tell me what she had said. But she wasn't spilling the beans, and I wouldn't pry.

She looked straight ahead as we crossed the green. "I wish William would meet a gracious lady. Someone he could spend time with so he wasn't so lonely."

I looked at her and stopped walking. "Why do you think he's lonely?"

Lily started walking backwards, putting distance between us and the Sweet Spot. "The love of his life died. They had no children. Do you ever see him around town, other than working at the bakery?"

I thought about that, and she was right. "No. I don't."

She poked a finger into my chest. It didn't hurt, but I rubbed it anyway to pretend it did.

"Exactly my point. So I asked him to have dinner with

me tonight." A pleased look radiated from her face, and her eyes gleamed with mischief. "If you're free, you can join us. We're going to meet at the Clam Bake at six."

That was why he smiled. He had a dinner date with a beautiful woman. "Sounds good. I can pick you up if you'd like?"

Tipping her head to the side, she seemed to consider his offer. "That's okay. I'm picking William up."

"In your Mini Coop? He's a tall guy. Are you sure he'll fit in the passenger seat?"

Her eyes roamed from my toes to hair. "You're the same height. I recall you fit just fine."

She had me there. I liked it when we cruised up the coast road in her bright-blue and white car. Especially when she put the top down. She looked cute with her hair all tousled. And the dark oversized sunglasses she wore made her face look like a pixie.

Snapping her fingers in front of my face, she said, "Earth to Gage."

An easy grin filled my face. "Sorry. Lost my train of thought."

"Looked like a nice one. Anyway, are you going to meet us there?"

"Of course. Thanks for including me."

She faced her shop. "We both have work to do, so I'll see you tonight."

I handed her the coffee, and she passed the bakery bag to me. "You can have both. If we're going to the Clam Bake tonight, I need to save room." She smacked her lips together. "Yeast rolls, lobster, and all that butter."

I leaned in to give her my customary kiss on the cheek when she opened the door to her shop and took a step over the threshold.

"Don't forget. Six." And then the door was closed, and she flipped the OPEN sign over.

For a moment, I was stunned. Lily never ... never what? She was going to work and here I was standing like a love-struck fool on the doorstep. Maybe William was right and I should listen to my heart and put it on the line. The worst that could happen is she wasn't in love with me. Or she could say she was and then where would we go from there? If it didn't work, it could end our friendship. I was about to walk away when I heard Lily scream my name.

I burst through the door, and she was hovering in the doorway to the back room. "Lily, what happened?"

Tucker was lying in the middle of the floor, facedown, not moving. I stepped around her. "Call it in to Peabody and tell her to send an ambulance." I bent over and felt for his pulse. It was steady. There was a nasty gash on the side of his head and blood soaked his shirt.

She nodded and made quick work of the call. I used my cell to take pictures of everything—the back door, the counters, and the area around where Tucker lay.

I could hear the tremor in her voice as she asked, "Is he dead?"

Chapter 13
Lily

My heart was in my throat as I watched Gage take a bunch of pictures. Shouldn't he be trying to help Tucker? I asked again, "Gage?"

"No. Tucker's unconscious. I don't want to move him with that head injury. And the bleeding seems to have stopped." I looked at her. "Are you okay?"

I nodded and said, "It just startled me. I wasn't expecting anyone to be here. Least of all someone like this."

He walked over and examined the back door, which was standing ajar. "No sign of forced entry. Did you leave this unlocked?"

I thought back to when I left the shop last night. "No. I'm always very careful about locking up." He snapped a few more pictures of the door and the lock.

"Did you touch anything when you came in?"

I heard the sharp tone in his voice and knew it was out of concern for me. "No. Well, except the light switch, and then I froze in place."

"Good."

I could hear the sounds of approaching sirens. This was

becoming too much of a routine thing. Tucker moaned. I knelt next to him, careful to avoid the deep-red circle under him. I placed a comforting hand on his shoulder.

"Don't move. Help will be here soon."

"I... Help me up."

"Wait for the EMTs. Gage is concerned your injury is more than that cut on your head." If I had been lying there, I'd want to get up too.

Under my touch, I could feel his shoulder relax. "I won't move." I glanced at Gage. "Can you check the rest of the shop?"

He said, "I'll direct the EMTs back, and then we can do a walkthrough."

After he left the room, I knew I had very little time. "Tucker, what happened?" It was in poor taste to question an injured man prone on my floor, but if someone had thought this was me, I needed to know.

"I came around the back to talk to you. I got a call. Someone said you were hurt, and I rushed over. The front door was locked, so I thought of the back door. It was open. When I stepped in, I felt a searing pain, and that was it until I heard you and Gage talking."

"Okay. We'll talk again." I moved aside as emergency personnel came into the small room and I went back to the front. Gage was just coming down an aisle of books.

"It looks all clear." He nodded his head in the direction of the back room. "What did he say?"

The man knew I wouldn't have wasted a minute before asking questions with Tucker being conscious. And me asking questions as a friend would cause the man less anxiety. I relayed the information, and his forehead's worry lines creased. "What do you think? Are you a target?"

I had already considered the plausible scenarios. "No. I

was the excuse. Tucker was the target, but whoever did this wanted him found. I don't think they wanted to kill him. This was a warning, maybe to Tucker or me." For now, I didn't share that in my bones I felt Tucker was a major piece of the puzzle. I just wasn't sure how. Yet.

Dax strode into the bookshop. With a curt nod to Peabody, who walked in ahead of him, he walked directly to where I was standing with Gage. "Detective. Lily. What happened here?"

He had an accusatory tone in his voice. I found his condescending attitude out of line. "I opened the shop and made my way to the storage room, and that's when I discovered Tucker lying on the floor bleeding from a head injury."

Dax's penetrating gaze was unnerving. "I noticed by the sign on the door you open at nine; it's almost ten. Were you running late today?"

"Gage and I met outside before I opened, and we walked over to the Sweet Spot for coffee." I pointed to my still full cup on the wooden counter. "You can see it's still warm if you want."

His brow shot up. "Do you make it a habit of opening the bookshop late so that you and Gage can meet for coffee?"

I didn't like the way he put extra emphasis on the sentence. Gage opened his mouth. I could defend myself, so I placed my hand on his. I could handle this insufferable man.

"Occasionally." I wasn't about to expand on my answer. It was none of his business and totally irrelevant to what had happened.

He shifted his attention to Gage. "I would guess you surveyed the scene, took photos, and checked the rest of the property?"

"I did. The back door was open, and it was intact. Lily is certain she locked it last night when she left for the day."

"Who has the keys?" He withdrew a notebook that was like what Gage had used when asking questions.

"My aunt Mimi. There is an extra at my place, and I think that's it." She snapped her fingers, and the sound caused Dax to look up. She suppressed a smile. "And my best friend, Nikki Twing. She works for me from time to time."

"Do you have her address and phone number?" His pen was poised over the pad, waiting for her to give him the details.

I rattled off the requested information. "I can assure you Nikki would never hurt a fly. She and I both believe in doing no harm to anyone or anything." I didn't bother to fill in that it was a witch thing. He might just slap on cuffs, thinking I was nuts.

"Thank you." He walked away without going any deeper in the conversation.

I turned my back on him and faced Gage. "That man is infuriating. How can you stand working with him?"

Gage looked over my shoulder. "In my job, we don't have the luxury of picking who we work with. Sometimes luck just isn't with us."

I knew I was lucky. Having grown up around the Cozy Nook Bookshop, it was logical that I took it over when my aunt had been ready to retire. And now it left me the freedom to follow any clues that might come my way.

"What's that smile for?" Gage was grinning. "Are you thinking up some way to get under Dax's skin?"

With mock indignation, I said, "Not at all. I would never poke at a law enforcement official, local or federal." I leaned forward. "We really need to find out what he's actually doing here."

"I know, but there are so many layers to that mystery." His eyes gleamed. "Maybe you should put your skills to work breaking that case and leave Teddy's murder alone. I'm concerned the phone call and Tucker being assaulted was a direct threat to you."

With a dismissive wave, I said, "That couldn't be further from the truth. I was used to get him here. I think whatever was supposed to happen went wrong."

He placed his hands on my upper arms and looked me square in the eyes. "Promise me you'll be careful."

I nodded. "You don't have to worry about me, you know. I have a few tricks up my sleeve." Not that the spells I had learned so far would help in all situations, but it had come in handy when I thought Gage was going to be the next victim at the library.

"One of these days, will you tell me about your tricks, as you call them? Like, did you take self-defense or something?"

"I've been reading a book Aunt Mimi gave me on practical things that will help me in life." That was the truth, too. Just not in the way he might think. "I appreciate that you care, but I'll be careful, and you're never more than a phone call away."

Before we could continue our conversation, the jangle of the gurney bumping over the threshold reached my ears. I moved to where Tucker was strapped in, the side of his head covered with a large square of gauze. He held up his hand, and I took it.

"Lily. I remembered something right before I got hit. A woman's voice. I don't know what she said. I can't remember, but it was definitely a woman."

Giving my hand a firm squeeze, I promised I'd lock up his store and put a note on the front door. "I'll check on you later."

He closed his eyes and gave a slight nod. "Thanks, Lily."

The EMTs rolled him out of the shop and into the back of the ambulance. On the bright side, Tucker was going to be okay. And the bigger point, I was sure a woman had killed Teddy. Now to figure out who.

I pulled into William's driveway at five thirty on the dot. He was a stickler for details and being on time was sure to be one of them. With a tap of the horn, the side door opened, and he waved and grinned before hurrying down the driveway.

Once he was settled in the car with the seat belt buckled, he said, "I can't remember the last time I went out to dinner and with such a charming young lady."

I felt the warmth rush to my cheeks. Partly because I felt bad that I had never thought about William being lonely before and partly because he said I was charming. If he thought so, maybe Gage did too.

"I'm glad we're doing this. It's high time you have dinner with friends." I pulled out of the drive. "Gage is going to meet us. I hope that's okay."

He rubbed his hands together and looked beyond happy. "Excellent. The more the merrier. Tell me what your favorite dish is."

I laughed. "Everything. But tonight, I'm going to have the lobster special. It's two crustaceans with rolls and lots of melted butter. If I get lucky, they have the best mud pie."

A twinkle in his green eyes made me wish I hadn't mentioned a great pie. After all, he had the bakery. "Oh, good. They still have that. Maybe we can share a piece. If I remember, it was enough for more than two. That's what Lulu and I would do. We'd each get a steamed lobster and split the pie."

"Gage and I always split it." My heart skipped. It had almost sounded like we were a couple, like William and Lulu. In my dreams.

"I talked with Jerilyn this afternoon. You stopping in gave me the prod I needed to reach out."

"Oh? How is she doing?" I slowed down so I could really concentrate on each word.

"She said she plans on coming back to work in a couple of weeks. She needed to get through the funeral and hopes to settle a few things with Teddy's cousin."

Then maybe she had seen a lawyer like I suggested.

"I mentioned you were asking about her, and she said when I saw you at the bakery next to pass along to you that your kindness doesn't go unnoticed."

"Did she say when the service was going to be held?" I planned on going. Maybe some of these questions about the mystery man, aka Jake Morrow, at Teddy's house last month would be answered. All I needed to do was find out more about him.

"Next week, she thought. It seems the cousin is taking his time making plans."

All of this was good information. "Did you get her address? I'd still like to send her a card."

"I should have asked her when I had her on the phone." He turned slightly in his seat. "You know what was odd? She didn't sound all broken up when she was talking about the funeral. When I was planning my wife's service, the tears were like a torrent. But she sounded almost..." He paused seeming to search for the right word. "Detached."

That was very odd. "Grief is a funny thing, and from what I understand, we all handle it in different ways. Maybe you caught her at a good time."

He nodded. "I'm sure you're right." Settling back in his seat, he said, "She asked how Tucker was doing from this morning. I guess the small-town express was in overdrive with that tidbit."

"I talked to Tucker before I picked you up. He's home and resting comfortably, and he mentioned Beatrice was going to bring him dinner and stay the night. The doctor wants him to be woken up every hour just to make sure he's okay."

"She's a good person. She was a good friend to Lulu too, while she was sick." His eyes grew misty. "They were best friends, you know."

"I didn't know that." A thought crossed my mind about William and Beatrice. But I'd talk to Aunt Mimi first. It was sad to see two nice people alone when they could spend time together.

Gage's car was in the parking lot, and I tucked the Mini Coop next to his. "William, are you ready to tie a bib on and get messy?"

My hand was resting on the gear shift, and he placed a hand over it. "Maybe tonight could be the start of a new tradition. I haven't felt this happy in a long time."

"I'm glad. I wish we'd done this sooner, too."

With a catch in his voice, William said, "Having dinner with you and Gage makes me think if Lulu and I had kids, they'd be like the two of you." That twinkle came back into his eye. "But you shouldn't look at him like he's your brother. I think there's something special between the two of you. I've seen that look before, you know, when I fell in love with Lulu."

"William." Once again, heat flushed my cheeks. It was like he had a window into my heart. "There'll be no matchmaking tonight. Understood?"

"I won't need to do anything. That spell has been cast."

His choice of words was very interesting. Did he know about the witches of Pembroke?

"Love is magical, Lily. For a woman who is so good at figuring things out, you can't see the answers to all your questions are right in front of you." He bobbed his head toward the windshield.

Gage was standing in front of my car. He came around to my side and opened the door. "Right on time, and they're not too busy." He looked from William to me. "Is everything okay?"

"Yes. William was just saying that we should make this a monthly event. Dinner with the three of us." I looked over at my new, older friend. I hoped he wouldn't continue the thread of our conversation.

"Yes. We should do this once a month and try different restaurants in town. It can be our supper club."

Gage held out his hand, and I took it as I slipped from the car. He said, "That's the best idea I've heard all day."

My heart quickened. Maybe William was right. Now all I needed to do was take a chance. The three of us strolled to the door. William had gone in first, and Gage was holding the door for me when I heard a deep groan from above us. I looked up, and Gage pushed me forward as the oversized neon sign fell, crushing Gage under its bulk.

Chapter 14
Lily

I looked right and left. There was no way to get around the sign safely and I didn't want to crawl over the top of the sign where Gage was pinned under the weight of it and I would not add to it. I could hear him groaning and it tore at my heart. How was I going to help him?

"William. Call for help." I raced down the hallway and burst out the side exit door. The emergency exit siren wailed.

When I reached Gage, I saw the twenty-foot-long wood and steel sign had landed squarely on his chest, pinning his arms down. I bent over to lift it off, but it was dead weight. What might have weighed a hundred pounds felt like one thousand. Too bad my adrenaline didn't kick in like I had always heard it would.

I knelt on the ground as close as I could get to him. Thank heavens I could see he was still breathing. "Gage. You hold on. William called for help."

His eyes fluttered open. "I'm gonna be late for dinner." He gave me a weak smile. "I didn't know signs were so heavy. Too bad it's not like that pen you were messing with."

I looked at the length of the sign. Was I able to lift something that large and if I could, would I be able to hold it long enough for someone to pull him out? My eyes locked on William's and he inclined his head. Did he know about me?

"I'm coming around. Wait." The older man disappeared inside.

"Are you in much pain?" I forced my voice to remain steady.

Gage's face was becoming paler by the second. Was he bleeding? "No. It just feels like an elephant is crushing me."

"Now, how do you know what that feels like?"

He gave me a tentative smile and his eyes fluttered. "Educated guess."

William touched my shoulder as he asked, "How is he?"

I stood. "I'm not sure. There's no way to tell how bad his injuries are with that sign on top of him."

"What are you going to do about it?" His green eyes never wavered. "You've got this."

"How do you...?" The question died. It didn't matter. "I can try, but can you pull him out if I can lift it high enough?"

"I lift flour sacks daily."

That was enough of an answer for me. I took a deep breath. "Gage. We're going to get this off you, but I need for you to close your eyes and concentrate on the pain being gone. Can you do that for me?"

He looked up. Concern washed over his ashen face. Things were changing quickly, and I didn't have time to think about if I could do it. I was going to get this sign off him.

"You'll get hurt."

I got on my knees and placed a hand on his forehead. "Do you trust me?"

"With my life."

That simple statement gave me the courage to stand, but not before I kissed his cheek. "Close your eyes and be ready for William to pull you out." In my head, I knew I wouldn't fail. I'm not sure where the certainty came from, but it was there. I closed my eyes. Silently, I said over and over, *The sign is weightless and chainless. Now it must hover until Willian can uncover. This is my wish, so shall it be.* After the third time, I opened my eyes and the sign was a couple of inches above where it rested on Gage's body. I didn't lose focus by speaking to either of the men. I gave William a nod and continued to focus. *The sign is weightless and chainless. Now it must hover until William can uncover. This is my wish, so shall it be.*

William put his hands under Gage's shoulders, and with a mighty heave, he slid him out from under the sign. In my mind, I let go of the wood and metal. It hit the ground with a loud crash. The sounds of the sirens were growing closer.

I knelt on the ground next to him. "Gage. How are you now?"

His eyes opened and the first thing he said was, "Are you hurt?"

"I'm fine. Really."

"Thanks for wrangling the elephant. I'm not sure how you did it, but—" He attempted to sit up, and I pressed a hand against his shoulder, easing him back to the pavement.

The door to the Clam Bake burst open and Fred Wickshire, the owner, started yelling. "What happened? Gage, are you okay?" Fred never did anything quietly.

William stepped closer to the man. "Fred, he's going to be all right. The sign came loose and landed on him, and he's free of the sign, and the EMTs will be here in a minute." He had done an excellent job reassuring Fred, who was looking at his building and the ground.

"I do not know how that happened. The sign company was out last week checking on it. They said it was sturdy and they had no concerns."

Gage held up his hand. "Call the company."

I took his hand. "There's plenty of time to take care of all that. For right now, we need to get you checked out." But what I was thinking was first Teddy, then Tucker, and now Gage. Was anyone safe in our little seaside town?

"Call Dax."

I must have frowned. Gage said, "Please. This could be related, and the town police officers are going to take this personal. I need someone who is impartial and can look at this with fresh eyes."

I wanted to argue the point more on me not trusting Dax, but Gage was right. We needed someone without bias. I looked around for my handbag, and William handed it to me without a word.

Digging to the bottom where the phone was, I looked up his contact information and dialed. He answered before the first ring had finished.

"Dax Peters." His tone was clipped but professional.

"This is Lily Michaels. I'm with Gage at the Clam Bake, and there's been an accident. Can you come out here? It's on Route One A."

"Is anyone—?"

I didn't let him finish the question if anyone was dead. "No. Gage was hurt, but I think he's going to be okay."

"I'm on my way." The line went dead.

"He'll be here soon." I looked at William. "How long before the ambulance will get here?"

"Patience. I know it seems like an eternity, but it hasn't even been five minutes."

That was hard to believe. Had time slowed, or was it just in my mind? I sat closer to Gage and kept holding his hand.

He said, "I know what you're thinking, but stop. This warning needs to be heeded."

"It was an accident. Nothing more. Not to worry, I'm not getting any ideas."

With a grimace, he closed his eyes and said, "I'll believe that when I see a blue moon."

"Now that you mention it, I heard there will be one next August. How about we plan on sitting on the beach and watching it together?"

"That's a date I'm going to hold you to."

Slamming car doors and the sound of people running caused me to look up. Once again, Peabody and Mac arrived together.

"Holy cow," Peabody said. "Did the sign land on the detective?"

I wasn't about to answer, as it was too close of a call. William said, "Yes. They talk about bursts of superhuman strength. Well, you're looking at the result."

Peabody said, "It's a good thing you were here, Mr. North."

He shook his hand. "I didn't lift the sign. Lily did."

She swung around to me. "You?"

I caught sight of the ambulance careening into the parking lot. I was saved by the rescue squad and the irony wasn't lost on me. "Gage. I'm going to get up and give the EMTs room to check you out."

He clung to my hand. "Remember, we have a date."

I smiled. "Yes. We have a date for next August."

I stood back from the growing crowd of emergency personnel and police officers. When one of their own was down, all bets were off. William walked over to where I was and put his arm around my shoulders.

"You did a good thing, Lily. Your hard work is showing."

"How did you know?" I shivered despite the warm jacket I had on, and William pulled me closer to him.

He dropped his voice. "Lulu was a witch. She always said you had the gift. I've been keeping my eye on you, and I can see your confidence has grown as of late. You've been practicing."

"For about a month now. Gage doesn't know." My heart hammered in my chest. "You won't tell him, will you?"

"It's not my place. You'll know when it's time." We both watched as they moved Gage to a stretcher. "The trembling is the last of your magic relaxing from such a strenuous effort."

I gave him a questioning look.

He bobbed his head in the direction of the sign. "Lulu was always drained after casting a spell, and she rarely did something extraordinary like that."

"Do you think he'll ask questions?"

"He might. But for now, pass it off as the rush of adrenaline. As a mortal, he'll accept that as the truth. But be prepared for him to be angry when you tell him."

I caught Peabody scanning the large group of people that had gathered. She crooked her finger in my direction. I hurried over to where Gage was on the gurney. It had been pulled to waist height. I assumed it made it easier to roll over the pavement.

"Lily." His voice was soft, but his skin color was better now that he was off the ground. Or maybe it was being against the stark white sheet that made him appear so.

"I'm here."

"Will you come to the hospital?"

I heard his voice crack. "Where else do you think I'd be? Certainly not having pie without you. I'm going to drop William at home first, and then I'll be along."

He nodded and whispered, "Thanks."

I bent over and brushed my lips against his cheek, lingering there, thanking the stars he was alive.

As they rolled him into the back of the ambulance, I could have sworn he said, I love you. But it was just wishful thinking.

"Lily." Peabody was at my side. "He was lucky. The EMTs don't think anything is broken. He's going to be bruised from stem to sternum, but he's alive." She glanced at the sign lying in front of the door. "How did you pick it up enough so William could pull him out?"

"You wouldn't believe me if I told you." I realized that had come out curt. I gave her a small smile. "Determination and focus."

"If I ever get into a tight spot, I hope you're around to save me too." She moved away.

That was the friendliest conversation I'd ever had with her. I looked up to where the sign should have been, only to see Dax walking gingerly over the flat roof. He crouched down and looked at the support posts. His brow wrinkled, and a deep frown appeared on his face. That was not a comforting expression. I ignored the surrounding hubbub, willing him to look at me again. When he did, he shook his head and shrugged. What did that mean?

William touched my arm. "Are you ready to go to the hospital?"

I looked at him, still distracted by Dax. "Almost. I told Gage I'd drop you off and then meet him in the emergency room."

"I can go with you if you want company."

"No. Thank you, but I don't know how long it will take and I know for a fact you're up before the birds, baking for the residents in our little town." I forced a smile to my face in the hopes he'd understand I needed to be with Gage.

"As long as you agree to a rain check for the three of us and dinner. It will give me something to look forward to."

He was a very sweet man. "Just try to skip out on us now." I threw my arms around his neck and hugged him tight. "Thanks for everything, William."

We moved to my car, and it shocked me to discover how close the sign had come to our cars. Just a couple of feet in a different direction and they could have been crushed. I shuddered again. Gage might have been killed. Or me.

"Lily," Dax called to me. "Wait up for a minute."

"He sounds ominous," William whispered.

I dropped my voice and said, "That's his normal sunny disposition." I turned to Dax. "Hey. I was just on my way to the hospital."

He glanced at William as if trying to decide what to say next. "Can I speak freely?"

"I'll wait for you in the car, Lily." William got in the passenger side and closed the door with a firm thud.

Dax took a step away from the car and the few people who were close by, and I followed him. When he seemed satisfied we were far enough away, he said, "This was a deliberate act, but I think Gage was just the unlucky person. The support posts were cut, and it was only a matter of time. I think the vibrations of the door opening and closing often were the final straw."

Dumbfounded, I felt my mouth drop open. "Any idea when?"

"I'm not an expert in this sort of thing. I'll need to bring in someone from Portland, but in my estimation, fairly recent."

I twirled around and paced the sidewalk that ran the length of the building. What was going on in our small town? What would happen next? I came back to where Dax stood, watching me.

"You're sure Gage isn't in any danger?"

"Obviously, I can't say for certain, but I think he was in the wrong place at the wrong time."

I shuddered to think if that had been a family and if it had struck a child, they wouldn't have been so lucky. Dax might not be best friend material, but I didn't think he'd lie to my face.

If it's related to what happened with the murder and Tucker being assaulted, I had to figure this out. I was wasting time.

"Lily."

I heard the warning tone in his voice. I thrust up my chin. "You have nothing to worry about. But when I call to say it's time to arrest someone, you had better be ready with handcuffs."

"You should leave this to law enforcement," he said, again with the hard tone, even if it was laced with a smooth Southern drawl.

"Secrets have a way of coming out, Dax. I intend to bring them to light." That wasn't just about this situation, but also about him personally. I was tired of all the nonsense going on in my hometown.

He cocked his head and stared. "Lily, should I take that as a personal warning?"

I returned his look with one of my own. "Just a statement of fact."

Chapter 15
Gage

The moment Lily entered my hospital room, the knot in my stomach relaxed. Knowing she was really okay was the best thing for me. I pushed the button on the bed and the top portion moved into a full upright position.

"Gage. Lie back in that bed. I saw the doctor on the way in and he said you're staying the night for observation."

"I thought you could drive me home." I certainly didn't want to stay here overnight. There was too much darn noise.

"Tomorrow, I'll be happy to. Tonight, not a chance." Her smile reached her eyes, and she looked around the room before sliding into the only chair next to his bed. "I talked to Dax before I took William home."

I shifted in the bed and cringed at the stabbing pain in my midsection and chest. The doctor had said he'd never seen a luckier man. To have gotten away with bad bruising and no broken bones or punctured organs was a miracle. But it was going to leave a mark for the next few weeks.

She jumped up from the chair. "What do you need? A nurse?"

"Stop. I'm fine." I placed my hand on her arm. "Tell me what Dax said."

"Good news. He doesn't think this was intentional toward you. It could have been anybody." Her shoulders drooped. "The bad news. It was deliberate. Someone cut through the supports, and it was a matter of time until it fell."

"What? I don't get it. Why would someone want to harm a random person?"

Her brow arched. "What if all this real estate stuff is a part of what's happened? The Davis corporation is buying up property. The Clam Bake has been waterfront for over fifty years, and that's prime real estate. A catastrophic accident might just force them to close their doors. The insurance company would pay off the claim, but the damage to their reputation might cause the business not to survive."

That seemed far-fetched to me. Why would someone want to hurt the Wickshire family? "I don't know. Maybe someone has just gone around the bend and is looking to get their sick jollies." My head was hurting, and this was more than I wanted to process at the moment.

"No more talk of what happened." Lily got up and straightened the blankets over me. "I promised William we'd get together for dinner as soon as you're feeling better, and I think it's something we should do every month. He's a lonely guy, and I feel like we bonded tonight over all that happened."

"That sounds like a plan." And if it meant I could spend time with Lily, in an environment that is more date-like, then all the better. "Do you think we could ask one of the single ladies in town to join us? Give him someone with similar life experiences to chat with as well. Who knows, maybe he'd even start doing more other than work."

Lily perched on the side of my bed, and I moved my legs to give her more room. "I'm not sure who we'd ask."

"Beatrice springs to mind, or Gretchen. They're both in their upper fifties and he's what? Around sixty?"

"I think so. But before we go setting up William with either of those women, they need to be in the clear about Teddy's murder. Right now, I'm leaning toward Gretchen being the killer. However, there's still the matter of Jake Morrow, the man I saw at Teddy's. I saw him on Main Street at the time of the accident, too. By the look on his face, he was horrified."

Gretchen was not my main suspect, and Lily was right about Morrow; we needed to know more about him too. "Why do you say Gretchen is at the top of your list?"

She thought for a minute. "Teddy had severely damaged her bank account. She wasn't getting the contracts he was. Without contracts, her sales dried up as did her commission. That wouldn't make for a friendly rivalry. Take into consideration she had access to the sales data, and she could figure out what he was doing. Gretchen is a smart woman. Teddy was spending money, and just look at the ring he bought for Jerilyn. That was not from the Cracker Jack box."

"All good points. But what about the gunshot? How could she have shot him without anyone witnessing it?"

She beamed. "I'm glad you asked. With a .22 handgun, it's something you can stow in a tote bag, even with a silencer. I noticed Gretchen carries a leather satchel. From my online research about the dimensions of the bag and a gun with a silencer, it would fit in there nicely."

I had to admit, I never noticed what she carried for a

purse. But Lily's observation skills were excellent, so I would take her word for it. "What about Beatrice?"

"She's lower on my list since I can't seem to find a motive, but she was standing outside her shop when I came out of mine. She could have watched him driving down the street and taken the shot. Everyone in town knew he always drove through town on his way to the beach most mornings."

"How did I not know that?"

Her smile was calm. "You're always at the police station kicking off your shift, but I'd wager there isn't one business owner on Main that didn't know his schedule, and that could easily be extended to customers too. You know some of those places have regulars, like the bakery, even the hardware store."

I nodded. She made excellent points. "What about the new car, and what would Beatrice's motive be?"

"Jill knew he bought a new car, so it must not have been a secret and he did love to flaunt his things." With a lift of her shoulder, she said, "Maybe Beatrice is a case of rejected love? Maybe she learned of Jerilyn and Teddy's romance and was secretly in love with him. If she couldn't have Teddy, no woman could."

"Would you kill a man over something like that?"

She leveled her gaze at me. "If I was in love with a man, he wouldn't want to look at another woman, and the entire world would know it."

I shifted on the bed and tugged at the collar on my T-shirt. Lily had a few points right, at least as far as this man was concerned. I didn't need to look at any other woman, and from what William had insinuated, he knew I was in love with her as did her aunt Mimi and Mimi's new husband, Nate.

"Tomorrow, I'm going out to the motel to talk to Monica. There has to be more about that Jake Morrow. He's the guy who's been staying out there, saying he was getting acquainted with his cousin. When I get back, I'll fill you in."

"I don't like the idea of you going out there alone." A shiver raced up my spine. "Why don't you pick me up when I get discharged and we can go out there together?"

Crossing her arms over her chest, she said, "Nope. I can almost guarantee you'll be on orders to go home and rest when you leave here."

I didn't want to fight with Lily. Changing the subject was the best course of action. "Who do you think hit Tucker over the head?"

"It was a woman, and I'm not sure why, unless he saw something the day Teddy died and doesn't realize it."

"He has been running around trying to convince not just me but anyone who'll listen that he had nothing to do with it. As if their bad blood was only an issue for Teddy."

"When I looked at the numbers, the difference between the assessed value and the sale price, if there was a kickback, wasn't huge. Maybe Tucker was the one guy Teddy didn't mess with."

"If that's the case, then he has no motive." My eyes were growing heavy, and I was fighting to keep them focused on Lily.

She leaned over and softly kissed my cheek. "You rest, and we'll spin more theories tomorrow."

Exhaustion washed over me. Or maybe it was the medication I'd been given, but I couldn't seem to form the words to say good night. I felt the bed rise as she got up. And then it was like a switch flipped off.

At nine o'clock the following morning, I was wide

awake and waiting for Lily to arrive when my phone chirped. It was Dax.

On my way. Coffee?

I responded with a grin along with a doughnut and a coffee mug emoji. Hopefully, he'd get the hint. I wondered why he was coming to the hospital. Could he have news about what really happened last night? As I rested, my nurse, Jane, bustled in, checked my vital signs, and announced the doctor would be in late morning. If he agreed, they would discharge me.

"Mr. Erikson, I looked over your chart this morning, and it is a miracle that you're alive." She put her stethoscope around the back of her neck. "Much less, no internal bleeding or broken ribs. You should play the lottery. I bet you'd hit the jackpot." She took one last look around the room. "Breakfast will be in soon. But if you need anything, just push the call button."

I thanked her and turned on the news. But other than the usual, nothing exciting was happening. I flipped back the covers and hung my legs over the side, waiting to make sure I caught my breath before standing. I steeled myself for pain when Mimi Michaels, Lily's loveable aunt, bustled in.

I was always taken aback at how much they looked alike except Mimi's hair was long and graying to a shade of silver which set off her sable-brown eyes. "Gage. What on earth are you doing?" She plopped her oversized tote on the hospital tray and waved her hands. "Back in bed."

"I was going to get my pad and pen from my jacket." I gestured to the slim closet across from the bed.

"I'll do that. It's a good thing I got here when I did." She slid open the door and within seconds withdrew the pad and a pen and held them up triumphantly. Not that it was that big of a deal, but if it made her feel good to help, then so be it.

She handed them to me, and once I got back in bed, she fixed the blankets so they were over my legs again. "I know how hospital food is, so I wanted to bring you some break-fast." From inside the tote she withdrew a ceramic covered dish and handed me a fork and a napkin. "Scrambled eggs, fruit salad, crispy bacon, and Nikki's specialty, apple cran-berry muffin." She waved her hand and mumbled some-thing I didn't catch before she announced, "Dig in."

When I pulled off the top, my mouth watered. This was far superior to a doughnut and coffee that Dax would bring, and suddenly, I was ravenous. "Thank you, Mimi. This was very sweet of you."

"You will not heal quickly if you don't eat. I expect you to finish every bite, too." She sat in the chair. "And I'm not leaving until you do."

I was happy to oblige as I forked up the creamy scram-bled eggs and crunched on the bacon. "How did this make it here as if you had taken it straight from the stove to my mouth?"

Her eyes twinkled. "That's my secret. Don't forget the muffin. Nikki would be devastated if you didn't finish that, too."

I grinned. "You don't have to remind me twice." After my plate was clean and the bacon, fruit, and muffin were gone, I patted my belly. "I feel better already."

Mimi packed up the dish and stored it in the tote before setting it aside. "Tell me about last night."

"I am assuming Lily called you and filled you in?"

"She did. I'd like to know what you saw and heard."

Aunt Mimi was adorable, another sleuth on the case. Of course, I'd give her my side of the story. Well, at least what I remembered. "Lily, William, and I were going in the door. I held it open for both of them." I looked out the window, trying to remember what happened next, but it was blank. "Mimi, I'm not sure. I think I heard Lily scream, and I felt this enormous weight on my chest."

She gave me a sympathetic nod. "Go on."

"Lily told me help was coming and I needed to focus. But I'm not sure on what. The next thing I knew, the weight was off my body and she was next to me, telling me I was going to be fine." Now I remembered how calm I felt when she was talking to me. "It was as if, with Lily beside me, nothing bad was going to happen. I felt protected." I could feel the color flood my cheeks. What kind of guy blushed when he admitted something like that?

She patted my hand. "Good. But do you remember anything else?"

I paused and tried to replay the events in my head, but I came up blank. "No. I can say I'm glad it was me and not Lily. I don't know if she could have withstood the sign. From what everyone has told me, I'm some kind of walking miracle."

Lily walked in the room just after that. I knew from the look on her face something was troubling her. She was clutching the pendant she had been wearing for the last few weeks. For a split second, I thought it surprised her to see her aunt, but she said, "Thanks for coming down."

"Of course. I brought breakfast, and Gage polished it off like he'd never seen food before."

She gave Mimi a quick hug. "Since you're here, I thought you'd want to hear the update."

Behind her, Dax was hovering in the doorway, holding a white bakery bag and a cardboard tray with what smelled like a sip of ambrosia. "I got here just in time."

Lily whirled around. "What are you doing here?"

He nodded to me. "Bringing my partner the cop special."

She gave a snort. "I just learned that you're not a fed at all, but a private investigator on the trail of heaven only knows what."

Dax let out a long, loud chuckle. "Good to know some things hold up."

Lily crossed her arms over her chest, and fire burned in her eyes. "What does that mean?"

He stepped inside and closed the door firmly behind him. "Have you ever heard the word undercover?"

She gave him the hairy eyeball, and I wouldn't want to be on the other side of that look. Been there. Done that. "Which part, the fed or the PI?"

"I'm definitely a federal agent." Dax looked at me for help, and I shrugged. This was between him and Lily and, for the moment, not my issue.

Lily tapped the toe of her shoe on the floor. She looked at me and Mimi and then took the bag and tray from Dax. She set them down and jabbed him in the chest. "You're coming with me."

Chapter 16
Lily

I marched down the hall, into the stairwell, and out the front door. I knew Dax would follow me, if for no other reason than his curiosity would get the best of him. I strode over to the small stone bench away from the entrance. "Have a seat."

Dax said, "I'd rather stand."

With a quirk of my eyebrow as if he was going to challenge me, I pointed to the bench. Darn, I wish I knew a spell to sit his butt down. But the stink eye would have to do the heavy lifting.

He tipped his head as he agreed and took a seat. "What do you think you know?"

"That you're a federal agent here to investigate something much bigger than Teddy Roberts. He's a pinprick in the boat you're trying to keep from sinking. I only said that stuff about being a private investigator to get you to come with me."

Dax said nothing to confirm or deny what I was saying. I stamped my foot, frustrated at his silence. What could I say to get him to show his true colors?

"Look. Like it or not, I'm good at solving puzzles. I'm pretty good at observing people and discovering what they might not want me to know. This makes me an asset to what's going on in town. My town."

"I know you like puzzles. But true crimes aren't like a board game or book."

For criminy's sake. I looked over the parking lot, and a large white truck was pulling around to the back side of the hospital. That's it. "You're taking care of our laundry problem."

His eyes flickered with appreciation and went back to remaining static. "I didn't realize the laundromat was having issues."

I had to remind myself to be patient. He really couldn't confirm or deny what I figured out. "Does Gage know?"

He lifted his shoulder in a noncommittal answer. Which I took as a yes. I snapped my fingers. "The Davis Corporation. Now it makes sense." I had been looking at this all wrong. I paced as Dax continued to sit and watch me.

"Teddy's been undervaluing houses for this corporation and taking kickbacks. Some people he's cheated discovered it and one of them could have taken matters into their own hands to stop him. I don't think whoever is behind the scheme would want it to end, so it had to be someone Teddy swindled. Unless Teddy got greedy, but I doubt it. He wasn't that smart. But why hit Tucker over the head and leave him in my shop? That makes zero sense." I looked at Dax. "How am I doing so far?"

"I can't wait to see where you're going, so please contin-ue." He crossed his one leg over the other knee and leaned back on the bench, appearing to make himself more comfortable. Even with that, he was tense. Dax's emotions rolled off him in waves like at the height of a storm.

"Gretchen was furious with what Teddy was doing, and either she wanted in on the action or she wanted to stop him. She was there the morning of the accident, and she carries a large tote, big enough to conceal a weapon. Of course, Tucker and Beatrice were also standing outside their shops and maybe they could have shot him too." I stopped pacing. "Jerilyn was on her way into the bakery. I wonder what she saw. I should ask her."

"No." The word came out like a low growl. "You need to stop asking questions."

I gave him a side-eyed look. "That means I'm on the right track." I dropped to the bench next to him. "Agent Dax, are you worried about me?"

He leveled his gaze to meet mine. "You have no idea how dangerous people can be."

A chill raced over me. I took the pendant in my hand, and it was overly warm. That was not a good sign. Usually it's cool, like it's just hanging around. The warmth had indicated in the past it had work to do, specifically to protect me. Was I in danger from Dax? I got up and moved away from him. Gage would never have let me come out here if I could even remotely get in trouble.

Confidently, I said, "I am on the right track."

"Did you hear what I just said?"

"Of course." I pointed to the hospital entrance over my shoulder. "One of the people I love most in this life is lying in a hospital bed. If things had gone the other way, he could be in a morgue right now. I will not sit in my bookshop, waiting for you to solve this case. Helping is all I can do." I took a step in his direction and then another. There was a lump in my throat. I grabbed his hand, surprised at the warm and instant connection I felt. I hung on as if he were a life preserver. "Please tell me you understand."

"I never said I didn't. But these are dangerous people and you're not equipped to defend yourself."

"I can. You don't need to worry about that." I thought of my big book, the one I should have been studying every day, but once again, it had been put aside to deal with this mess. "I won't take any unnecessary chances."

"Lily. I admire your tenacity, and heck, I even might like you just a little." He smirked. "If you tell anyone I said that, I'll deny it."

"I'm not sure if I like you either, but Gage trusts you, so I guess by default, I kind of do."

"Thanks for the vote of confidence."

I stepped back and tugged my hand free. "But this doesn't mean I'm going to stop thinking about the case, and people will tell me things they won't tell you. It's a matter of trust."

"Agreed. But they will talk to Gage. He's a local like you."

I smacked my forehead with my hand. "You still haven't confirmed what happened last night. Do you think someone wanted to cause harm?"

"I'll say this. I don't think whoever did this wanted anyone to get seriously hurt or worse. But do I think it's an attempt to close the restaurant's doors? Maybe. They're sitting on oceanfront property. If you could get that at a bargain price, what a coup."

I mused, "We were just in the wrong place at the wrong time."

His expression was somber. "Yes. I shouldn't be telling

you this, but the preliminary report indicates the storm we had a few nights ago must have sped up the incident. Which is why I'm here. I was going to fill Gage in."

I nodded as I felt the wind rush from my sails. In a good way. Neither Gage nor I were the targets. "Is there any way to tell when it should have toppled over?"

"No."

The finality of his word struck me to the core. The implications were endless. But there was no sense in dwelling on what might have happened and didn't.

"I'm going to talk to Gage about this. All the business owners in town need to check their buildings and confirm they're all safe. Another accident is avoidable if we all remain vigilant."

"Good point. I'll ask my uncle to come and check my place." Actually, if Aunt Mimi was still visiting with Gage when I got back, I'd ask her to have him stop by when he had some time. I trusted him above anyone else in town. Especially in times like these. "Dax, thank you for coming out here with me so we could talk freely. I won't hang around long so you can fill Gage in on the details."

"I can drive him home if you'd like. I know you have things to do today." He smiled. "Bookshop things."

I couldn't help but laugh at his attempt to clarify I was to steer clear of sleuthing. "We can talk about that upstairs."

After I closed the bookshop and before I was going to run by Aunt Mimi's for dinner with Gage, I headed out to the motel. Monica said she was working until eight and had some information for me. I approached the office door and looked up and down the façade of the building. A few cars sat in front of the doors, and I wondered if Dax had made it back yet. But I didn't see the dark sedan anywhere. Not that it mattered, but curiosity had always been my Achilles' heel.

Opening the front door, the cool interior air hit me in the face. Why did Monica have the air conditioner on? The temperature was dropping outside. She looked around a large computer screen and grinned. "Hey there. Glad you could make it."

"I'm glad you called. Why is it so cold in here?"

Laughing, she said, "It discourages guests to stand around and chat when I'm busy. I've kind of gotten used to it being about sixty in here."

I rubbed my hands over my arms. "Brr. I won't stay long."

She stood up and flicked open the counter so I could walk behind the desk. "You have to see this. The last time you were here, you were talking about Jake Morrow. And I got to thinking. I have a ton of security cameras all over the place. I've been scanning through them, and I found a couple of interesting recordings. And don't worry, once you're done with the preview, I'm going to call your detective and fill him in."

"Can you reach out to Agent Peters? Gage just got out of the hospital. He had a small run-in with a sign." I wouldn't elaborate since Monica obviously hadn't heard the news yet.

"Sure, I can do that." She sat back down and started tapping the keys. "Give me a second."

I started watching the screen. I leaned in closer. "Who's Teddy with? He looks vaguely familiar."

Monica thrust her hand through the air, triumphant that she had something good on the screen. "That's what I was talking about. Teddy is walking with Jake Morrow."

She rolled the chair closer and tapped a few keys. "Hold on, there's more."

"What are they doing together?" The time stamp was the night before he was killed. The men seemed to have fun, joking around, having a grand old time. As they stood there talking, the parking lot lights came on, and Teddy handed a book to Jake, then gave him a hearty guy kind of hug with a back thump and then a handshake.

"They certainly look like they're good friends," Monica said. She clicked the keys a few more times. "This was the day of the accident." Jake was coming out of his motel room, and he was wiping his eyes with a handkerchief he pulled from his back pocket. He was definitely crying.

"Can you back this up? Was this the first time he came out of the room?"

"I knew you were going to ask me that, and yes. Based on the footage after Teddy left, he went inside the room and didn't come out until now. His car never left the space in front of the room."

Based on this, the likelihood of him killing Teddy was slim, but I saw him in town. Unless he walked. I know I saw him that morning. The only other time I had seen Jake, he was sitting with Marshall, Jill, and Teddy at Teddy's place.

"Thanks for showing this to me, Mon. Is it possible I can take a picture of the screen? I want to ask Marshall if he knows what Jake's relationship is to Teddy. It only makes sense he'd know since they were together at least once before."

She stopped the video, and I could get a pretty clear picture of the screen. "Call Agent Peters, and don't tell him you showed this to me first. I don't want him getting cranky with you."

"I heard he's not bad looking. Thinking you might ask him to dinner?"

My head snapped around. "No. He's not my type."

"Tall, thin, dark eyes and hair. It doesn't seem like he'd be too hard to have across the table." She winked. "You're not dating anyone, are you?"

"If you're interested, you ask him out. With my full support."

Monica's smile filled her face. "Gee, thanks. I just might do that if he comes in to see the video."

"Ask him to. I'm sure he will." I put my hand on her shoulder. "Just remember he's only here temporarily, so if you were to get attached, it might lead to a broken heart."

"Thanks for the info, Lily. I'm just looking to have some fun. All I do is work."

I knew exactly what she meant. For me it was practice spells, the bookshop, and trying to solve this murder.

"We should do a girls' night. Talk to Nikki. We can go for pizza, or even better, Robin's Café for dinner. We can kick back and relax. Eat some good food, maybe have a glass of wine too."

"That sounds good. I'll talk to Nikki and we'll make a firm plan." I looked at my phone, trying to decide if I had time to run out to Marshall's place, but I was supposed to be at Aunt Mimi's five minutes ago. Maybe after dinner, I could convince Gage to go with me. He might feel like he was still involved, even though his accident had put him firmly on the sidelines.

I hurried to my car, calling thanks as I went. With a quick glance over my shoulder, it felt as if I was being watched. I looked around, and the curtains fluttered in the room that belonged to Jake Morrow. I debated for a fraction of a second before striding to the door and giving it a firm knock. When he didn't answer, I hit it again. *Bang. Bang. Bang.* Still no answer, and I didn't hear anyone moving around on the other side of the door. What I heard was the sound of tires chirping as it struggled to gain traction on the driveway from gravel. I watched the late model pickup truck speed past the motel and at the very last second, the driver turned. Jake Morrow.

Chapter 17
Lily

By the time I got to Aunt Mimi's, I was fuming. There was a back exit, probably a window, so Jake Morrow could have snuck out of the motel, pulled the trigger, and made it back to be on security video, crying like he had just heard his favorite person in the world was gone. I stormed in the back door and slammed it shut.

Gage, Aunt Mimi, and Nate's heads swiveled in my direction.

"Bad day?" Gage asked.

I held up my hand. "The last hour." I snapped the strap of my bag on the hook inside the door with my coat next.

Nate spoke. "It's rare you come in like a gale force wind. Tea?"

Mimi whispered, "Chamomile." He nodded and moved to the stove.

The table was set for dinner, but with the knot in my stomach, I knew I couldn't eat a forkful, at least not until I calmed down. Closing my eyes, I slowly counted to ten. When I opened them, Gage was watching me.

"Are you going to tell me what happened?"

Nodding, I said, "I was at the motel talking to Monica." Ignoring that suspicious glare, I continued. "Do you remember Jake Morrow?"

"Yes, he's one of our suspects."

"It turns out Monica has a bunch of video footage with the two of them together. At first, I thought he couldn't have killed Teddy over a bad business deal because I saw the two of them acting like they were best friends. And the day Teddy was shot, Jake came out of his motel room wiping his eyes."

"I don't see your point."

I scooted my chair closer to him. "He was in the town square that morning. When I was leaving the motel, I felt someone watching me, so I looked around and the curtains in his window fluttered like someone had pulled them back."

Gage closed his eyes and put the palm of his hand against his forehead. "Please don't tell me you confronted him?"

"I didn't."

He exhaled. "Thank heavens."

"Because he peeled out of the parking lot in a truck, which means he had to have gone out a window. I checked with Monica and there isn't a back door." I smacked my hand on the wood table, causing the plates to rattle. "He could have snuck out, killed Teddy, and gone back to the motel with no one ever seeing him."

"You're right. That could have happened, but the more important question is, did he see you tonight?"

I nodded. "Of course. It wasn't dark out. I'm sure he saw me knocking on his door and that's why he slipped out. Every time I think I've taken someone off the list of suspects, they just hop right back on. I'm never going to figure this out."

"Lily."

There it was again. That disapproving tone. "Gage." I made sure I dragged his name out, just like he did with mine.

A small flicker of a smile tugged the corner of his lips, and then it was gone. "You run a bookshop. You're not a police officer."

I waved my hand. "That's irrelevant. Dax can hardly know about local connections." I perked up. "After dinner, would you care to take a little ride with me?"

As much as I was excited, Gage looked dejected. "I'm afraid to ask, but where are we going?"

"Out to Marshall's farm. I want to show him the picture of Jake and ask him what the connection is to Teddy."

His eyebrow quirked like Spock's did. "If I say no?"

"Then I'll drop you at your place and head on out to the farm."

He groaned. "You know I'm suffering from injuries that are only twenty-four hours old."

If he was looking to play the sympathy card, it worked. "You're right. I'm sorry I asked. I'll definitely drop you home before I head out to the farm." With that settled, I patted my midsection. "I'm starved."

When Gage didn't respond, I looked at him. "What?"

"You are the most exasperating woman I know."

I grinned. "I'll take that as a compliment." I went to get up. Aunt Mimi had slipped into the kitchen with Nate, and I would help put dinner on the table so I could get out to the farm.

"I will ride with you. As long as there's no creeping along foundations and running to hide, that is?"

I wagged my finger in front of his face. "One time. I did that once. I should never have told you."

"Ah, but you did and now look, you're still following up on that night by tracking down Jake Morrow, who, for all you know, is just an average guy who was Teddy's friend. Nothing more or less."

I popped my hands on my hips. How could he be so blasé about this lead? It was the best one we've had in a while. "If he was innocent, why did he take off tonight when I knocked on his door?"

Gage blinked. I had him. "Hungry?" I said sweetly.

Driving inland toward Marshall's farm, I glanced at Gage. "You're still up for the ride along?"

He nodded after being strangely quiet during dinner. Pleasant conversation had flowed, but mostly between Mimi, Nate, and me. Maybe he was exhausted. We had filled the last day or so with a lot of activity.

"It won't take long. You're going to show Marshall the picture. He'll answer your questions and we can head home."

Ah. The word *home* trailing from his lips conjured up a nice thought. What if they were going to her home together? Like as in an actual couple. Not just buddies. Had William been right about speaking her mind? But there was the whole witchcraft thing to figure out. I could talk to Aunt Mimi about how she broke the news to Nate and, more importantly, how he took it. That was the ticket. She would seek expert advice.

A few more miles slipped away, and Gage had looked at me several times. His forehead wrinkled as if he were wrestling with a tough question, the meaning of life, or something just as serious.

At last, he said, "I remember all the details about last night."

I took my eyes off the road and glanced at him. "Some of that would probably be best to forget. I'm sure the pain was intense. I know from where I was, you were so pale, and I was terrified."

"Is that how you did it?"

My heart thudded in my chest. I knew exactly what his question referred to, but I wasn't prepared to be honest. Not yet. We both needed to be in the right headspace to have that kind of conversation.

"Did?" I let the question hang in the air. Playing dumb never worked for me, but there was always a first time.

"Dax told me the sign weighed a couple hundred pounds. You and William together might have been able to lift it. But I saw you. You were concentrating and talking to yourself. I felt the heavy weight on my chest. And another minute later, the weight had vanished, and William pulled me out and the sign fell to the ground. I know somehow you got that sign off me."

I took a deep breath. My voice needed to be steady. "You know what people say. In times of extreme stress, a person can do amazing feats. I just picked it up, and William did the rest." I clutched the steering wheel a little tighter. "How else did I get it off you? And as far as muttering, you know I talk to myself all the time. I was psyching myself up to get the job done."

He stared at me. "Tell me the truth, Lily."

I slowed the car and drove under the sign that said Marshall's Farm Stand.

"I am." I was being honest. I needed to convince myself I could move the sign, and I was saying the spell over and over. I stopped the car and put it in park. Turning in the driver's seat, I looked Gage square in the eye. "I would have moved mountains to get that sign off you. I've never been as scared as I was last night. William gave me the confidence to try, and together, we accomplished what needed to be done."

I could see he wanted to believe me wholeheartedly. He dropped his gaze. "I was scared too. It was the first time in my life I felt truly helpless. And for a split second, I thought it would have been better if I was the person getting help instead of needing it." Tears welled up in his eyes. "What kind of person thinks that way?"

I leaned over the console and did my best to wrap my arms around his neck, being careful not to put any pressure on any part of his body. "An honest one. You're trained to help people, and last night you were on the other side. It was only natural to wish it had been different. But I know you, maybe better than you realize. And you would never wish any harm to come to anyone. We're alike that way." I kissed his cheek. "And the next time, you can be the hero. It's too much pressure for me."

I saw the beginning of a smile light his eyes. "You'll always be my hero, Lily."

"Good." I pressed the palm of my hand to the curve of his face. "Now can I go be Jessica Fletcher?"

In a light teasing tone, he said, "Who am I supposed to be in that scenario?" The twinkle was definitely in his eye now.

With a laugh, I said, "Why Amos, of course."

A sharp rap on my window caused me to jump. "What the heck?"

Marshall was standing outside the car. I opened the window and gave him a tentative smile. "Hi, Marshall. Do you have time to talk to us for a minute or two?"

He stepped away from the door so I could get out, and Gage got out of his side. Marshall nodded at Gage. "Evening. Heard you had an accident last night. I'm surprised to see you up and about."

"How did you hear?"

"Small town. Fast grapevine." He was wearing a pair of coveralls that had a healthy dose of dirt on them. He soared past six feet and with the sleeves pushed up, it was easy to see the muscles he had earned from hard work. The deep creases in his weatherworn face were enhanced as he smiled at us. "But you already know that."

Ever since I discovered he cared for Jill Dilly, he had gotten more at ease around me. I was glad since I really liked Marshall. He was a true gentle giant.

"Isn't that the truth?" Gage said. "I was wondering if you would look at a picture Lily has. I'm hoping you know who he is."

"Be happy to." He pulled his reading glasses from the inside pocket of his coveralls and slipped them on.

I had my phone out and was ready to show him the picture. He took the phone and after a couple of seconds, he said, "That's Jake. Teddy's cousin. I met him a couple of months ago. We've been playing poker at Teddy's every couple of weeks. A good guy." He handed me my phone.

"Teddy's cousin? Any idea what he's doing in town?"

"He said they hadn't seen each other in years and spent some time catching up. When Teddy first introduced us, he said his cousin's name was Tommy, but he said we should call him Jake since he preferred his middle name."

I scrunched up my nose. I was not buying that. "Didn't that seem odd to you?"

Marshall stuck his hands in his pockets after putting his glasses away. "I guess Jake was his middle name. I'm not sure. But he's a pretty good guy and a terrible poker player. Even Jill beat him a bunch of times. Not that she's a terrible player, but he was boasting how good he was. It was funny to see her knock him down a couple of pegs."

I smiled at the idea of Marshall sitting beside her, silently cheering her on. I gave him a playful hip bump. "Have you asked Jill out to dinner or even coffee yet?"

Bright crimson flushed from his collar to the top of his head. "Timing's been off. Outta respect for Teddy, I'm going to wait until after the funeral. But I'm going to do it. Promise. This is another reminder life won't wait for us to stop pussyfooting around. I don't want to miss my chance to spend time with her."

"Good. I can't wait to hear how it goes." He got an encouraging smile from me. I held up my phone. "Thanks for clearing this up."

"You're welcome, and you'll be the first person I tell after we make plans." He held up a hand to Gage. "You take care of yourself now. It's good to see you've got a driver for while you're getting the job done. Lily's a fine woman."

Before Gage had to respond, I said, "Have a good night, Marshall, and if I don't see you before, I'll see you next week at the funeral."

"Drive careful going home." He nodded. "Moose."

We got in my Mini Coop, and I did a three-point turn before heading back down the driveway. "So, Jake is Tommy, also known as cousin." I didn't have to ask. Gage was already calling Dax.

"Hey, it's Gage, and I'm with Lily. I've got you on speakerphone so we can both talk. We just got confirmation that Jake Morrow, who's been staying at the Coastal Motel, is really Tommy Jake Morrow, Teddy Roberts's cousin."

"How did you do that?" His voice held his usual surly tone.

"Lily had a picture on her phone, and we showed it to Marshall Stone. Turns out they've been playing poker every couple of weeks at Teddy's place."

"Any idea what he's doing in town?"

"No. But any chance you can run his name and picture? I can send you a text."

"Yeah. Not sure how long it will take unless he's been up to some unsavory stuff, but shoot it over and let me see what I can do."

"Thanks."

"You said Lily can hear me?"

"I'm here, Dax." This wasn't about to be good news.

"How exactly did you get that picture?"

The jig was up. He knew and was waiting for me to confess. I would not skirt the truth, but he didn't need to put me on the spot. It was just a power trip for him. I decided I wasn't going to give him the satisfaction.

"Does it matter?" I smirked at Gage, who shook his head and tried to suppress a grin.

"It does if you tampered with evidence."

"I did nothing of the sort. Last I checked, watching videos wasn't against the law."

"Lily, if you altered anything you saw, it will not keep you out of trouble just because you could get some important information and we're friends."

I did a cutting motion across my throat. "What's that, Dax? You're breaking up." I grinned. "I can't hear you…"

Gage depressed the off button. "You really are something else."

I flashed him a saucy grin. "You have no idea."

Chapter 18
Gage

Lily dropped me at my place after driving into town. I convinced her I didn't need a babysitter tonight. The doctor had given me medicine to help me sleep, and I was going to take it.

Once I got settled on the sofa, my cell rang, and it was Dax. When I answered, I was expecting him to be annoyed but was surprised when he sounded happy.

"Gage. Interesting news. I checked out Thomas Jake Morrow. He and Teddy Roberts are cousins. They haven't seen each other much since Morrow's been working in Alaska for the last twenty-plus years. From what I can tell so far, there was no animosity between them, and he has zero real estate investments. His lifestyle is modest."

My mind raced with possibilities. "You're not liking him to be the murderer?"

"No. I still believe it's tied to the fraud and money laundering case I'm working. And another thing. I overheard him talking to Monica, the owner of the motel. After the funeral and once he wraps up a few things with the sale of Teddy's house, he's heading back home."

Had Dax discovered any more family who might show up? "Anyone else who could inherit his estate besides his cousin Jake?"

"That will depend on his will. Teddy may have made provisions for his future bride, but we won't know that just yet."

I heard a snap of fingers, and Dax said, "Lily mentioned Jerilyn was upset as Jake wasn't letting her take part in the final arrangements, and she was going to contact her lawyer to see if she had any sway. Do you think Lily could somehow find out how that went?"

His train of thought surprised me. "I thought you didn't want her involved because of her being a civilian?"

Several seconds went by, then Dax said, "I realize she has a sharp mind, and I'm okay if we use her more like an informant."

That wasn't what I wanted to hear. "Informants have a way of getting into trouble when things go bad. They get caught in the crossfire, and I'm not comfortable with that."

"Jerilyn doesn't pose a risk. They're friends, and all Lily is going to do is follow up on a previous conversation."

Dax had a good point, but I didn't have to like it. "I'll talk to her tomorrow and see if she can help."

"Good. And how are you feeling? I still can't get over that you didn't come away with serious injuries from the sign. You and I both know blunt impact can kill."

I gently rubbed my tender ribs and chuckled. "I'm like Lily's cat with nine lives." Thinking back to the accident, I said, "I'm glad it was me and not a young kid. They wouldn't have been so lucky. Any working theory on that? You had said the supports were cut."

"We found a couple more buildings with recent repairs

and a couple of them were accidents waiting to happen too. Electrical issues at the Sweet Spot was one."

I sat up straight. My heart hammered in my chest. "William's place. Did you tell him?"

"Relax. As soon as it was uncovered, we told him. He got an electrician right over, and it's been fixed. Before you ask, the Cozy Nook Bookshop is scheduled for tomorrow."

The man knew what I'd ask next. Dax was an excellent agent and colleague and maybe even a friend. "Thanks. I appreciate knowing you're taking care of her, too."

"She has a good heart, and I like her."

I heard that statement, and it was loaded with a question. Was he interested in her as more than a casual acquaintance?

"Do you know if she's seeing anyone?"

"Um. No."

"No, like she's not seeing anyone or you don't know?"

My gut tightened. "She's not dating."

"I'm thinking of asking her out to dinner after we wrap up this case."

Was the man asking my permission to date the woman I loved? "Yeah, great." My voice was strained. "She's the best person I know."

He paused. "Are you okay with me taking her to dinner?"

At least he was getting the hint this wasn't the best topic of conversation for me. "Of course." The words were like sand in my mouth. "If you're asking her out to pass the time…"

"No. That's not my style. When she commanded me to talk to her out of your hospital room, I realized I wanted to get to know her better. Her mind, the way it processes information, is unique. And she's feisty. I like that."

I smiled. That was one way to put it. "There's no one else like Lily." I had a small hope that she wouldn't say yes. But we were friends and if she wanted to date Dax, who was I to object. Especially since I wasn't about to open my heart to her.

The next morning, I literally rolled out of bed. Having slept with the help of the pain medication the doctor had prescribed for a few nights, all my muscles were still stiff. My first thought was Dax asking Lily out for dinner. The tight feeling that had settled in my gut last night lingered. I got ready for work. My feet dragged as I walked into the kitchen. I had just put coffee beans in the grinder when there was a sharp knock at my front door.

I pulled it open, and Lily was holding up a cardboard box which held to-go containers. "Breakfast," she said, then gave me a wide smile. "Can I come in?"

Opening the door wider, I stepped aside, and she walked right into the kitchen. Over her shoulder, she said, "Silverware and plates, please."

"Um. What are you doing here?" I opened a cupboard door and took two plates, along with forks, to the table.

"We have a case to talk about, and I'm sure you're not feeling up to fixing a decent breakfast. So Aunt Mimi called and asked me to come by and deliver. When I got there, she had enough for both of us."

"Mimi doesn't need to continue to cook for me." But my mouth watered at the aroma that wafted up from the containers, so my protest was evaporating quickly. "She brought food when I was in the hospital, then dinner when I got out, and now this."

"My aunt believes food has healing powers, and she said

to finish it all." Onto our plates, she scooped oversized slices of quiche loaded with veggies, the pungent smell of cheese in the air. Next came chunks of fresh fruit and thick slices of homemade pumpkin bread. "Did you remember the jam?"

She gave me her stink eye and laughed. "Aunt Mimi packed her special blueberry jam and I'm instructed to leave the jar. But remember to save it once you've emptied it. She reuses them every year." She looked at the coffeemaker. "Have a seat, and I'll brew a pot."

"Lily. You don't need to wait on me." I added more beans to the grinder and gave it a whirl. She added water, and then I put the freshly ground beans in the basket. "Teamwork."

"The best kind of work," she agreed.

I took a step toward her, and she took one back. The electricity between us sparked. The way her eyes widened, I knew she felt it too.

"How did you sleep?"

It was easy to see she wanted to move the conversation to something benign.

"Not bad. Just muscle stiffness."

She pulled out a chair and sat down in what I liked to think of as her spot. "Aunt Mimi said it should be gone by tomorrow. She added some herbs to the quiche and fruit that will help ease it."

"It's come in useful she knows a lot about natural reme- dies." The coffee was brewing, so I withdrew the cream from the fridge and then the sugar bowl from the cabinet. Lily liked her coffee light with a touch of sweet.

"I think with Nate working so hard on the boat, she's learned a few tricks to help him so she's passing them along to me, and as an extra touch she sends along some of her special dishes to you too. I'm sure she added the herbs to all the meals you've had so far."

That was a curious thought. Was that why I was healing rather quickly, at least physically, from the accident? Now, my heart was bleeding at the thought of Dax asking Lily on a date. Would Mimi have something for that too?

"Gage?"

"I'm sorry. Did you ask me something?" I took the carafe and poured a large mug of coffee before finally sitting down across from her.

"Yes. I wanted to know if Dax called you about William's electrical issue?"

"He did. He said your store was going to be checked out today." I cut the quiche and discovered it was delicious. I didn't care what herbs it contained; it was amazing. "This is good."

She smiled. "I'll tell my aunt."

"Do you want me to be at the shop later when the people come to inspect it?"

"No. I'm sure nothing is wrong. If someone had been hanging around with mischief on their minds, I'm sure Milo would have told me."

I let that comment slide. Those two had a special connection. Not that Milo could speak actual words, but they communicated and, on that point, I was sure.

"When I talked to Dax last night, he wanted to know if you could speak with Jerilyn. See if anything came of her talking to a lawyer."

She nodded. "He called me this morning, and I said I would. I had planned on bumping into her today anyway. She asked me to locate an out-of-print book a while back on the history of Maine and it came in yesterday. I was going to call her when I opened the shop and see if she could stop in.

This way, we can have a casual chat about all kinds of things."

"What else do you plan to talk to her about?"

Setting her fork aside, she folded her hands on top of the table. "Gretchen's possible romance with Teddy. I was going through some old newspaper archives from when she opened her business, and guess who was standing next to Gretchen with his arm around her waist at the grand opening of her office?"

"Teddy?"

She nodded, and her eyebrow arched. "The one and only. From the looks on their faces, they weren't friendly business rivals, but that relationship was much closer to five years ago than last week."

I drummed my fingertips on the table. "That puts a new wrinkle on things. Scorched romance fuels anger and revenge."

"That's what I thought. And if Jerilyn knew about their past, I'll bet she could have some dirt that will lead us directly to Gretchen pulling the trigger."

"Tell me why you're so convinced it's her."

She pointed to my half-empty plate. "Eat, and I'll outline my working theory."

I was happy to oblige since every mouthful tasted better than the one before. "I'm listening."

"Patience." She got up from the chair and leaned against the counter. "I think better standing up."

I grinned. "Whatever works."

Clapping her hands together, she said, "I heard the crash and rushed out of the shop. I saw the car was smashed into the pole, and I glanced around. Someone needed to call for help. I noticed Beatrice, Tucker, Gretchen, William, Jerilyn, and Ross Frederick, but I ruled him out since he's only been here a little over two weeks."

"Then how do you know him?" My plate was empty, and with my belly full, I leaned back in the chair, sipping on my mug of coffee.

"He came into the bookshop looking for an area map. He's from Washington State and going to be a professor at the University."

"Kind of a tough drive in the winter if he plans on settling here."

With an impatient wave of her hand, she said, "We're getting off topic. I'm sure Ross isn't our guy, so let's move on."

I took a swallow of coffee and remained silent.

"I'm not sure if you remember, but Gretchen carries an oversized tote, something that could conceal a multitude of things, including a small gun with a silencer."

"If she was on Main Street, how could she have taken the shot with other people around?"

"Gretchen was just coming out of the walkway between Bee Bee's and Tucker's store. She could have shot him and then stepped into view."

"Good point."

"It was Beatrice who rushed back into her shop. Presumably to call for help as I rushed to the wreck. At that moment, I was still under the impression it was a basic car accident. While others came closer, Gretchen moved in the opposite direction, closer to the buildings. Watching, but not trying to help."

"It's circumstantial at this point."

"But you confirmed she has a permit for the same caliber of gun. You need to ask her for it and run it down to

Portland to see if it was the gun that killed Teddy. If it is, then you have your person. Case closed."

"Motive?"

"He was destroying her business and had started a new life with Jerilyn. Double rejection."

All of these were excellent points. "What about Tucker and Beatrice?"

She sat back at the table. "Like me, they heard the commotion and came out of their stores to see what had happened. We can be a bit of a busybody group."

"Then why didn't William?"

"Jerilyn was going into the shop, and she must have told him before she realized who it was. Then devastated, she went home to wait for word on who was responsible."

"Don't you find that strange?"

She tipped her head. "How?"

"If that had been me, would you have gone home?"

"You can't compare Jerilyn to me. She's more reserved than I am."

That was an understatement. The women were total opposites. Lily was ready to lend a hand, talk to anyone, and was very social. Jerilyn would have preferred to be part of the wallpaper. "How do you think she and Teddy got along?"

"They say opposites attract. From the outside looking in, they were very different. Maybe once they started dating, there were more similarities than differences."

I had to wonder. "And with Gretchen, they were two peas in a pod."

Lily smacked the tabletop. "Exactly. That's why I'm sure Gretchen is the killer."

Chapter 19
Lily

When I left Gage's house, I drove straight to the shop. I would ask Jerilyn to come down later this morning, and that would give me time to practice a spell or two with Milo watching over me. I wondered which one would be next.

"Milo," I called as soon as I closed the front door and flipped the sign to OPEN. "Time to start our day."

I hurried into the back room and noticed a couple of men through the window. "May I help you?" I said once I pulled the door open.

A tall, thin middle-aged man wearing coveralls and a CSI patch on the front said, "Agent Peters requested us to check your building for safety concerns, ma'am."

I nodded, deciding I didn't need to call Nate to check things over. "Yes. Do you need anything from me?"

"Not at the moment. But we will be inside in about fifteen minutes if that's all right?"

I told them I'd leave the door unlocked and went back inside. I stopped in the middle of the room. Remembering

Tucker sprawled in the middle of the floor with the door open, I bent over to examine the lock again. There were no scratches on the metal indicating a tool had been used to force it. Which meant there had to be a key. Would Gretchen have an old master key to these buildings? I remembered Aunt Mimi telling me that the gentleman she bought the building from had owned most of Main Street in the early days. As far as I knew, we had never changed the locks.

I went back to the front and dug my cell from my bag.

Without waiting to exchange our normal pleasantries, I dove right in to my reason for calling. "Hi, Aunt Mimi. When you owned the bookshop, did you ever have the locks changed or are they original to the building?"

"Lily. What's gotten you so fired up?"

Her soft, melodic voice calmed me. Was this another witch thing? There was no time to ask about that now. I needed to know about the locks.

"Tucker was hit over the head, and when I found him, the door was open. Someone had to have the key."

"You're correct. I never changed the locks. There was no need. Old Mr. Brooks would never have used his master once I handed over the check for the building."

I pumped my fist in the air. There was a master floating around out there somewhere. "Did he also own the Sweet Shop and maybe even the Clam Bake?"

"The bakery, yes for sure, the Clam Bake possibly. Check the registry of deeds. You can see who owned every building going back for years."

"Thanks, Aunt Mimi. You're the best." I hung up and there was Milo sitting on the counter. "When did you get here?"

"Just now. I knew you were having breakfast with Detective Cutie, so I didn't need to rush. But what are you so excited about? You're just about dancing in place."

"There's a master key floating around, and I'll bet Gretchen has it. That's how my back door was open. She lured Tucker here, smashed him over the head, and left the door open just as a tease."

He gave me a disdainful look. "Why?"

"It's called a red herring. Don't you ever read Agatha Christie books? It was to throw us off the trail of her as the murderer. She would never have known that we'd find out about the key. I have to call Gage and see if he's discovered anything about the gun."

Milo yawned.

"Am I boring you?"

"A little. I thought you wanted to work on your spells and here you are, concerned about who killed a man who was committing fraud."

I reached out and scratched behind Milo's ears. "I know I've been distracted and not working on my craft as much as I should be. We're so close to Gretchen being arrested. I'll be back at it soon, maybe within hours."

Milo stood on all fours and walked across the counter. My hand trailed down his back. "I'll be in my window seat until you're done."

I called after him, "I won't be long."

"Promises. Promises." With a flick of his dark-gray tail, he disappeared.

Now to call Gage and then Jerilyn.

After lunch I went over the spells I had already learned so far—lighting a candle, levitating my big book of spells, and finding it after Milo hid it, which he thought was an excellent lesson too. I wrapped up with my summoning spell for a cup of coffee. I was surprised to see William crossing the grass, headed in my direction with a small white bakery bag and a to-go cup in his other hand. Had I somehow summoned him personally?

He entered the shop, and I crossed to the front of the store to greet him with a warm hug. "William, this is a surprise."

He handed me the cup and bag. "I had a feeling you needed a pick-me-up, and I thought of something I had to tell you right away."

"You should have called. I would have come over." I tipped my head to the side. "But thank you. This is so sweet." I gestured to the wingback chairs near the large window. "Do you have time to sit for a minute?"

"No. I need to get back, but you need to know that two days before Teddy Roberts died, Gretchen Wilson came into the shop. Jerilyn was waiting on her and they bickered. At first, I paid no attention. I was checking on the cinnamon rolls rising in the proofer. When their voices got even louder, I went out front, and Gretchen was telling Jerilyn to mind her own business or she'd be sorry." He hung his head. "I'm sorry I didn't remember this before, but the shop has been so busy with being short-staffed and all."

He had my full attention. "Any idea about what, specifically?"

"I heard Teddy's name, and Jerilyn said something about buying a house. Other than that, no."

"Thank you for telling me."

"What are you going to do about it?" His eyes were full of concern. "If Gretchen is responsible for what happened, please don't confront her. Let Gage and that agent handle it."

"No worries. I don't intend on talking to Gretchen, but I'll let Gage know what you heard. He might come over to talk with you directly."

"If I'm not at the shop, he knows where to find me."

"Thank you for the information and the treat."

Now he beamed. "You're welcome, and did you take my advice about your detective?"

I shook my head. "Not yet. But I plan to."

Rubbing his hands together, he beamed. "Good." He left the shop and hurried in the direction he had come.

I pulled out my phone and texted Gage and Dax what William had just told me. That put a new wrinkle in things. A few moments later, I got a text back from Gage, but not in the thread with Dax.

Gretchen has a gun. A .22 caliber. Be extra careful.

I had been right. All that was left was to see what Jerilyn might know and fill Gage in so he could arrest her, and this would be over. Jerilyn could bury the man she loved, and I could tell Gage how I really felt about him.

Before I could take even a sniff of the coffee, the bell over the door tinkled. Jerilyn was walking in, dressed in deep shades of dark green with the most forlorn expression I had ever seen. She was struggling to come to terms with the loss of Teddy.

Jerilyn closed the door behind her with a firm thud. "Hi, Lily. Thanks for finding that book for me."

"It was my pleasure. You know me and puzzles." Inwardly, I cringed. The last thing I needed was for her to realize when we started talking that I was grilling her for details.

Her smile was weak. "True. For as long as I've known you, you've always been trying to solve something."

I held up the cup and bag. "Let me put these down, and I'll get the book from the back."

She nodded and walked around the bestseller table, her fingers trailing over the covers. "No rush. I have nowhere to be and no one waiting for me."

My heart broke at her grief-laced words. I located the book and went back to the front. Hoping to perk her up, I said, "Here it is, and it's in pristine condition, too."

She met me at the counter and took the book. Turning it over, she gave me a weak smile. "It is in excellent shape. Not that it does me much good now. I really wanted it for Teddy so he could see the history of our town. He only ever saw each building in dollars and cents. Not for what else it might represent."

She handed me her credit card, and I swiped it. Then she signed the slip of paper.

"I have been meaning to ask. How did you make out with the lawyer? Were you able to give his cousin some input on the services?"

She shook her head. "My attorney talked to the estate lawyer, and he can't reveal the contents, but they have notified everyone who is a beneficiary. The will is being read the day after the service."

"I'm sure that will be a relief to you."

Her head snapped up, and her eyes blazed with anger. "I'm not invited." Tucking the book in her bag, she stormed out of the shop.

I was stunned. Teddy hadn't made any provisions for his future wife. Why wouldn't he have changed his will if he was proposing?

My cell rang. It was Gage.

"Hey. I've only got a minute, but I wanted to tell you we're arresting Gretchen. So good work on talking through your observations this morning. That put her with opportunity and motive. Suddenly, her business has picked up. The competition is gone."

"Is there a chance whoever was working with Teddy on buying up property will contact her? And could she use that as leverage if she agrees to help Dax track down whoever was behind that scheme?"

"Potentially. I'll let Dax handle that. She'll be arrested for Teddy's murder. That is my primary concern, so the citizens of Pembroke can relax and know they're safe."

"Except for whoever clonked Tucker." I said that more to myself than to Gage. There was still the matter of the master key. "When you're questioning her, can you broach the subject of a master key for some of the buildings downtown?"

"Sure, but why?"

I took the top off my now lukewarm coffee and sipped. "Whoever has that old key is the person who assaulted Tucker. If it wasn't Gretchen, then we still have a problem on our hands."

"I'll find out and let you know." We promised to touch base later, and I offered to supply dinner if he was interested. It pleasantly surprised me how quickly he said yes.

Milo appeared on the counter, and I jumped. "Why do you do that?"

He did the lazy cat stretch. "Because I can." He rolled over on his back with his paws in the air. "Would you mind rubbing my belly? I have some things to tell you, and this is my reward for my information." He closed his eyes and waited.

I couldn't believe my familiar was holding information hostage. I groaned. "Spoiled is your middle name."

"But you love me. I've heard you say it many times."

I scratched under his upper legs. "That was before I found out you actually understood me."

He opened one eye and looked at me. "Not true. I hear you every night just before you go to sleep."

I refused to keep this line of conversation going when I needed to know what he knew. "Spill it."

"Well. Did you know Jerilyn is actually living in her parents' old house? From what I gather, she never moved out. Not sure if she's paying rent or what. I found that to be quite interesting."

I chewed on my bottom lip. What did that mean? "What else?"

"The night before Teddy's untimely demise? He and Jerilyn had a knock-down, drag-out fight."

"How do you know this?" I rubbed the top of his head and Milo purred. When he didn't answer me, I stopped. "Information, please?"

He opened both eyes and rolled to a sitting position. "I've told you before, there are enough familiars around. We all talk to each other, network if you will."

"Is Jerilyn a witch?"

"No. And for the record, not every person in town is a witch but we do have a decent size coven. Stop thinking we're going to wander around meeting a bunch of witches. We're not. That will come with your first coven meeting."

"Anything else of interest?"

"I haven't been able to discover who has the master key, but you're right, one exists, and I'll bet my next catnip mouse that all the buildings which have been tampered with have their original door locks."

That was something I could research. All it would take was a call to Dax. I dropped a kiss on the top of his furry head. "Milo, I adore you."

He answered with a low, cowardly lion kind of growl. "You better get busy. And I have some sunshine to sleep in."

I sent Dax a text message asking for the list of buildings with suspicious problems. Then I crossed the room and pulled a town map from the rack. I was going to plot what buildings had problems and see if it correlated at all to property Teddy had sold or that he wanted to sell. Somehow, this all tied together and if nothing else, it would tighten the handcuffs on Gretchen just a little tighter.

My cell phone pinged with a text from Dax. He had listed all the properties with issues that they knew of so far. It surprised me that my shop wasn't on the list.

Dax picked up on the first ring. "Agent Peters." His voice was gruff, and I could picture the scowl on his face.

"Hi. It's Lily."

"Hello. Will that list be helpful?" I could hear his voice soften after I spoke. What was that all about? Had we become friendly since our hospital chat?

"Yes. It's helpful, but I wanted to double-check. There was nothing wrong at my shop?"

"No. The investigators found nothing other than they think you have a mouse problem and suggested you get a cat to prowl around at night. Maybe leave Milo at the shop for a night or two."

I thought of my familiar and knew there'd be no way he was going to turn into a mouser. "I'll keep that in mind. Thanks for the suggestion."

"My pleasure." Again, his tone was peculiar compared to the other times we had talked. "Would you like to meet me at the Sweet Spot for a coffee tomorrow? I can wait for you outside around nine?"

I thought of how many times Gage had waited for me on the sidewalk, and that's when it hit me. "Dax. I have to go. Gage is about to arrest the wrong person for Teddy Roberts's murder."

Chapter 20
Lily

I needed to get to Jerilyn's parents' house and quick. "Milo," I called to him, but he didn't answer. When I rounded the corner to wake him, the cushion on the window seat was empty. I had zero time to track him down. I hurried back to the counter and sent Gage a message.

Gretchen's not the killer. Jerilyn knew Teddy was shot, and she was carrying an oversized tote bag going into the bakery after the accident. On my way to the Busch house. Meet me there. Hurry!!!

I grabbed my keys, flipped the front sign to CLOSED, and ran through the shop and out the back to my car. Before I jumped in, I heard Tucker calling to me, but there wasn't a moment to waste. If I was right, Jerilyn would leave town tonight once word of Gretchen's arrest hit the gossip train.

I approached the stately house high on the cliffs overlooking the Atlantic Ocean. It must have been amazing growing up here as a child. All those porches, widow's walks, and the views. I couldn't imagine what it must have been like to watch a storm rolling in from the east. Heavy cloud cover partially obscured the late afternoon sun. I momentarily watched the waves. They were an ominous dark gray-green as they pounded against the rocks. The pendant I wore around my neck grew warm. Danger was ahead, but I needed to summon the courage to talk to the house's lone occupant. I could stall for time. My mom used to say I could talk to a wrong number for hours. This would be a snap as long as I kept my nerves in check.

I parked and climbed the wide wooden steps to the front door. Distant thunder rumbled. I rapped on the door using the old black wrought iron door knocker shaped like a mermaid. I liked the touch of whimsy. The sound of muffled footsteps reached my ears and from the corner of my eye I saw a flutter of lace curtain. I exhaled. Jerilyn was still here.

The door eased open, and she peered from around the side. "Lily. I wasn't expecting you."

"Hello." I took a step closer to the threshold. "I wanted to stop by and see how you're doing. When you left the bookshop earlier, you were upset."

"That's very kind of you. I'm fine. Life has just been one shock after another."

"May I come in?" I glanced over my shoulder. "It's about to rain. I was hoping we could visit until it stopped."

Her eyes darted to something behind her and back to me before she eased the door a little wider. "Of course. We can have tea."

I entered the main hallway, and just as I suspected, several suitcases were sitting on a deacon's bench below a large ornate mirror. The stairs rose to the second floor. To my right was a dining room devoid of furniture and to my left was a living room with two long plush sofas, one facing an old fireplace and the other the front windows. I could see the ocean whipping the waves higher and the water spray crashing over the rocky shoreline. I gave a silent prayer that Nate was home and was safe from this storm.

"I'll be right back with tea. Make yourself comfortable."

She shook her head and said no when I asked if I could help. I withdrew my phone and checked for a text from Gage, but had nothing. I sent a quick note to Dax.

At the Busch house. Tell Gage to come quick.

He returned with *LEAVE!*

I put my phone on silent, enabled voice to record, and slipped it in my pocket as I watched the storm getting closer to shore. It was powerful and a bit unsettling. Despite having lived near the ocean most of my life, I knew the intensity of the waves, and it was unsettling to be this close.

A few minutes passed, and Jerilyn returned carrying a tray. It held two china cups rimmed in gold and a matching teapot. On the small plate in the center, a few shortbread cookies had been artfully arranged.

"This looks lovely," I said as she poured the tea.

With a glance over her shoulder, she seemed to check on the storm before handing me a cup. "Here you go. I don't have any milk or cream. I'm sorry."

I nodded toward her bags. "Going on a trip?"

She nodded. "I am right after the funeral. I need a change of pace. Pembroke has too many memories." She looked around. "This house, growing up and now losing Teddy, is just too much."

"It surprised me to learn you were still living here. I thought this was Teddy's first big sale?"

"It was. But I rented it. The whole thing went so quick it was over before I thought it through. The money was good, but I don't think we would have sold the house if things had moved more slowly." She nodded. "But what's done is done."

"Couldn't you have canceled the deal before closing?"

She shrugged, and a flash of anger slipped over her face and then faded. "Perhaps. But Teddy reassured me it was the best deal they would ever get for this old place." She looked around. "It has good bones, as my daddy used to say. Weathered many storms with minor damage. Even the biggest of hurricanes on record were more of a bump and run to this place."

I could hear the sadness in her words. It was as if someone had taken her best friend. "I didn't know this place meant so much to you. Did you rent it back from the new owner?"

"Something like that. I'm just borrowing it for a little while." She pointed to my cup. "Drink up, it will chase away the chill."

I sipped my tea, not that it had cooled. Jerilyn eyed me with interest. "How do you like it?"

"It's delicious, just hot." I set my cup down, and Jerilyn almost seemed disappointed.

"It's a special blend. Not like what your mother makes, but I've been experimenting."

I noticed the liquid in her teacup was much lighter than mine. "Aren't we drinking the same blend?"

"We are, but I like the first pour when it's just steeping. Yours went longer."

I was at a loss for words. I got up and crossed to the front windows. Where was Gage? "I'll bet as a child you loved to sit and watch the storms." I jumped when I realized she was standing next to me. "Oh. You startled me."

"Would you like to see the storm from the widow's walk? It's one of my favorite places in the house."

The gleam in her eye was not the warm and friendly kind. A shiver raced down my spine. I rubbed my arms as if I was cold. "You know, I think I should be going. Maybe if I hurry, I can miss the worst of the storm."

Jerilyn grasped my arm. "I insist. This will be your last chance to witness the raw power of Mother Nature."

Now that didn't sound inviting. I noticed her other hand was in her side pocket, and she withdrew a small handgun. "Walk with me. I promise before the storm unleashes its wrath, I'll be on my way, leaving you to enjoy the spectacular view." She jerked my arm, and she was surprisingly strong. I always took her as soft, more like underbaked bread dough. She half dragged and shoved me toward the stairs. I could feel the muzzle of the gun pressed against my back.

I walked deliberately up the stairs, hoping with each slow step it would give me time. I looked around, praying I would see something that could be used as a weapon. But they had cleared the house of all insignificant items. The first set of stairs was complete. One to go. I had to get her talking. Partly to stall and partly because I had to know why.

"Jerilyn, killing me won't bring Teddy back." Her grip was still like a vise around my upper arm.

With a short, almost diabolical laugh, she said, "I wouldn't want him back if he could rise from the dead. And where he went, he's dancing with the devil."

"I thought you were recently engaged."

She jerked me to a stop and held up her left hand with the enormous diamond. "I found this ring at his house. But it wasn't for me. He planned to worm his way back into Gretchen Wilson's heart. The ring was for her. That night before he died, Teddy had the nerve to break things off with me. After all I did to help him build his financial empire."

"Wait, what do you mean, you helped him?"

She tapped her foot and sneered. "Since you always have to satisfy your curiosity about everything, I'll tell you." She pointed the gun to the next set of stairs leading up. "Once we get outside. Climb."

My mind raced. If she was behind the fraud scheme, then Dax should be closing in on her as I took the steps. I stumbled halfway up. She jerked up on my arm, and I cried out. The pain in my shoulder burned. I reached over to rub it, and there was blood. What could I do? Jerilyn was crazy enough to kill me.

Still lying on the stairs, I realized she didn't hold all the cards. "Give me a second?" I closed my eyes and focused all my attention on Gage. In my mind, I asked him to come. *Find me. Hurry!* I remained with my eyes shut until Jerilyn must have grown tired of waiting.

"Let's go."

I scrambled to my feet, my boots slipping on the smooth wood treads. When we reached the top, she shoved open the door and threw me against the rail. I pulled myself tight up on the weatherworn posts. It jiggled slightly, and I looked down to see the boards were cracked and worn. I held on, walking around the outer edge. The wind tore at my jacket, and my bangs fell into my eyes. For a moment, I closed them and called to Gage. By the stars, he would arrive soon. She held the gun, and I had zero magic against that.

"You were going to tell me about how you helped Teddy make money?"

She pointed the gun at my midsection. "Stay put and I will."

I held up both hands. "I'm not moving." From the corner of my eye, I saw an old straw broom lying on the wood floor. Too bad I couldn't fly, not that it looked sturdy.

"Before my parents sold Teddy this house, at my insistence, I had a crush on him. I had for years. Not that he ever noticed me until I mentioned that we were going to sell the house. He jumped at the chance and the commission alone was more than he made in six months." A slow smile spread across her lips. "That's when I knew I could control him. Money is a powerful motivator. I introduced him to a friend who knew someone looking to invest in real estate." She laughed, and it seemed to echo in the wind. "No one ever pays attention to the frumpy woman behind the counter." She tapped her temple. "But because of me, Teddy got exactly what he deserved."

Fear wrapped around my heart.

"I'm really sorry, Lily. You have always been so nice to me, but I know you figured out that I shot Teddy. The car accident just added a bit of flair, don't you think?" She tipped her head and looked at the ocean and then back at me. "But I'm curious. When did you figure it out and what was the tip-off?" She waved the gun. "This isn't registered, so I know that's not a problem. But don't you find it amusing that Gretchen has a permit? That's why I got exactly the same kind." She leaned closer, as if sharing an interesting tidbit. "It will slow the police down, and I'll have time to get out of town before they find you and they'll never find this. It will be at the bottom of the ocean."

I opened my mouth and concentrated on moving the broom. If I could get it to move, I could draw Jerilyn's attention away from me. Maybe I could wrestle the gun from her.

"Don't be shy. I appreciate how your mind works. So tell me everything."

I could see the broom was beginning to wiggle, but I had to answer her. "I didn't realize you were the one until just a while ago. When you and Gretchen were arguing in the park, you let it slip that Teddy had been shot. At that point, no one knew. Also, you were going into the bakery right after the accident, carrying a tote bag. Not running toward the accident. If this was the man you loved, you would have been trying to rip the car door off with your bare hands."

She nodded and seemed to have an appreciative smile. "Excellent. Anything else?"

"Gretchen's gun wouldn't have matched the ballistics, so they would have ruled her out. Teddy's cousin Jake said he wasn't aware you even existed. Since they've been spending so much time together these last few months, why wouldn't you have come up? All the other suspects had airtight alibis. But I'm curious. Did you assault Tucker in my shop?"

Her grin was scary, as her eyes were now more like a crazy person and less like the woman I had known for years.

"Of course that was me. Teddy had a master key, which is how he had been tampering with some of the shops to devalue them. And Tucker had been running all over town whining. I was tired of it, so I thought that would make him think twice. And for the record, it worked. He finally stopped talking about being the potential target of the police."

While Jerilyn was talking, I focused every ounce of persuasion in the broom's direction. It was finally moving directly into my hand. When she saw the broom flying, her mouth fell open, and that was all I needed. I swung the broom as hard as I could, hitting squarely across her stomach. She dropped to her knees, gasping for breath. The gun slipped from her hand and was dangerously close to falling into the surf below. The door burst open. Gage, with Dax right behind him, ran out, both with guns drawn.

"Don't move!" Gage demanded. Dax moved in and hauled Jerilyn to her feet while Gage handcuffed her.

"She admitted she killed Teddy and more." I withdrew my cell phone and held it up. "I recorded it for you, too. Hopefully, it can be used as evidence." I pointed to the gun. "Based on Jerilyn's confession, that's the gun that killed Teddy."

She twisted away from Gage and glared at me. "Why couldn't you have just drunk the tea? I'd be long gone and you would have been dead before anyone found you."

"Jerilyn, you mentioned it. My mom blends teas. I knew at the very first sip you had tainted the tea. There was no way I was going to drink it."

A loud crack of lightning followed by rolling thunder filled the air.

Gage bobbed his head in the direction of the door. "Let's go."

Dax withdrew a plastic bag. "I'll get the gun." He looked me square in the eye. "Nice job."

Gage groaned. "Don't encourage her, Dax."

I smiled. "And you might want to know Jerilyn spilled more than just about Teddy. The real estate scheme is still going strong." I grinned at both men. "And for the record, I'm going to help solve that one too."

Gage said, "This wasn't enough excitement for you, Lily?"

"All I want to know is, what took you so long? I texted you and you didn't text me back."

It began to rain, and he said, "It was the strangest thing. I never got the text, but I was questioning Gretchen when I thought I heard you calling to me. I had to find you. I had

Peabody take over, and I left. Dax was on his way to the station. I guess you sent him a text. And here we are."

Dax took Jerilyn by the arm and walked her through the door. I put my arms around Gage and held him tight. It didn't matter now that the rain was coming down in sheets. I knew he could hear me when I called to him. My magic and confidence were growing stronger every day. "Thanks for coming to my rescue."

"By the looks of things, when I got here, you rescued yourself. All I did was slap on the handcuffs." He looked at the broom on the ground. "Did you use that to disable her?"

"I did."

"Lucky thing it held together."

I gave him a wide smile. "It wasn't luck, it was magic."

If you loved **Catnaps & Crimes** help other readers find this book: **Please leave a review now!**
Are you ready to read more from the Lily and the gang in Pembroke?
Keep reading for a sneak peek at
Tea & Trouble
A Book Store Cozy Mystery Series
Order Now
Or
Shop at Lucinda Race
Not ready to stop reading yet? If you sign up for my newsletter at www.lucindarace.com/newsletter you will receive an excerpt for Cookies & Capers, the introduction of when Lily met Milo right away as my thank-you gift for choosing to get my newsletter.

Tea & Trouble

Chapter 1 - Lily

Lily

I tilted my head back, face toward the early morning sun, and drank in the crisp fall air. It was a perfect day for the annual Pembroke Cove Fall Festival. Today I was reading fortunes at my parents' tea booth. I slowly twirled in my long deep-burgundy velvet dress. The hem of the matching cloak brushed the tops of my ankle boots as Gage Erikson, my best friend and hopefully someday my boyfriend, touched my hand. I wanted to look the part of a witch but I didn't want to wear all black. Aunt Mimi had found this dress in an old wooden trunk which had been tucked away, unopened, in her attic for years. The bonus, it was a perfect fit, as if it was made for me. I know my aunt thought it was kismet and even with being a witch, it didn't mean everything in life I touched was magical.

"Lily, you look beautiful." Gage's hand warmed mine and his smile was the real deal.

I did a mini curtsy. "Thank you, sir." I took a long look at what was supposed to be his costume. All the people working the festival agreed to stick with the theme of their booths. "What made you come up with dressing like a farmer in overalls and flannel?"

"I'm helping Marshall Stone with his stand." He pointed just across the town square. "I'll be right over there and we can make funny faces at each other all day."

I couldn't help but laugh at the way his eyebrows wiggled when he talked. "We're not twelve anymore." I hated those years were long gone twenty-five years ago. He twirled me again and this time he pulled me closer to his chest. He looked into my eyes with an intensity I hadn't seen before.

"After the last six weeks, I think we should go back to when we were kids and didn't have anything more to worry about than fishing and going to a movie at the Lights Out Theatre. Two murders and me getting crushed under that sign at the Clam Shack has been a lot to handle." Concern clouded his eyes. "And you did most of the heavy lifting."

I flashed him a cautious grin. I wasn't sure if he was referring to me levitating the sign off his body—which he still didn't know I actually did—or the fact that I was directly involved in solving the murders of Flora Gray and Teddy Roberts. With a nonchalant shrug, I said, "It was no big deal. I like puzzles and both of those incidents were a way to exercise my brain."

He leaned in and kissed my cheek like he always did while he said, for my ears alone, "My best friend is brilliant."

And there it was, the perpetual friend zone. Would Gage ever look at me as more than his friend? Probably not. This had been going on for years. Maybe it was time I started dating someone else. Possibly Dax Peters, the investigator who had come to town around the time Flora was killed. He seemed to be showing more than a passing interest in me lately.

Before I responded to his compliment, I noticed my parents headed in our direction. Dad was carrying a carboard box which would hold paper teacups and other supplies for brewing various teas and my mother had a tote bag slung over her shoulder with what I guessed would be her special blend. My aunt had told me Dad was a witch, but my mom wasn't. However, her tea blends were amazing, and today I would be reading tea leaves from a special blend she had created just for the festival. In addition, she had bags of other teas to sell in our booth.

I tugged my hand from his. "I need to help my parents. They brought more supplies for the booth."

"I'll come too." He fell in step beside me and it was just one of the reasons he was a good guy, always ready to lend a hand. "Did Mindy make her special blend again this year?"

I gave him a quick side-glance. "You never miss a trick, do you?"

He puffed his chest up and strutted a bit. "It's my job, ma'am, to notice the little details as a detective on Pembroke Cove's police force."

I laughed so hard a snort escaped. "Easy, Detective, you might strain the buttons on your flannel shirt."

My parents met us halfway, and Gage took the bag from over my mother's shoulder and the box Dad was carrying. "Hello, Reed." He gave my mother a one-armed hug. "Mindy." He looked at me. "Doesn't Lily look great in her witch costume?"

Dad's brow quirked at the word costume. Mom placed a gentle hand on his arm and said, "She looks amazing."

Mom reached out and straightened my modified witch

hat. "I like how you decorated the traditional black hat with burgundy lace and cutouts of teacups."

"A touch of whimsy, Mom." I linked arms with hers and we crossed the leaf-covered grass to our booth space. Parked behind the tables was a tiny silver camper from the 1970s. It was one my parents used every time they went to fairs in the northeast. Inside, we could heat water, get warm if the day was chilly, and if the day turned hot, cool off. And the best part was the fridge stocked with snacks.

Mom scanned the table setup. "I see you have everything ready to go."

"There wasn't much to do. You had it organized inside. All I had to do was flick out the tablecloth, put cushions on the seats, and set out the bags of tea that you want to sell." I held up one hand and announced. "Voila."

Gage said, "Just like magic."

I leaned closer to Mom, and she wrapped her arm around my body, and whispered, "He doesn't know."

She nodded and conveyed her understanding with a concerned smile. Mom had known for years I have been in love with Gage, even if he didn't. But I had come to terms with our relationship and for the most part accepted we would always be best friends even if it wouldn't lead to anything more.

"Looks like it's going to be a great day for a festival," Dad said. "Gage, are you joining us in our booth this year?"

"No, sir. I volunteered to work at Marshall's booth. His helper got food poisoning and Marshall needs an extra set of hands." He set the box and bag on the corner of the display table. "Is there more in the truck?"

Dad nodded. "Ladies, we'll be back."

They started off in the direction of vendor parking, and

Chapter 1 - Lily

Mom began to unpack the bagged tea. "Are you ever going to tell Gage that you care for him as more than a friend?"

I picked up a sleeve of paper teacups and began to set them up next to the bag of loose-leaf tea I would use for the readings. Longing to say yes, I instead looked away and said, "No. He doesn't think of me in that way."

Mom quirked a brow. "Are you sure about that?"

I looked at him walking next to Dad. "He's had so many opportunities and never said anything."

"Neither have you." It was a gentle rebuke, but I was a bit old-fashioned and thought the man should state his feelings first. Like Gage asking me on a real date. Not like the casual, *hey, let's have dinner tonight,* kind of comment.

"We're better off as friends. If we started dating, it might not work out, and then I'd lose what we have."

"That's not like you, Lily, leaning into the fear of something not working out. You've always been an eternal optimist." She smoothed my hair back from my face and searched my eyes. "Do you want to talk about what is really going on?"

Maintaining eye contact, I said, "I've made a decision to start dating. I might even ask Dax Peters if he'd like to have coffee with me." That went against my idea of dating, but those rules only applied to Gage.

Mom's hand cupped my cheek and she kissed the other one. "I think that is a fine idea. Get out there and have some fun."

I saw the sparkle that came into her deep-brown eyes as she spoke. "Mom, do you sense something that I should know?"

Her smile quirked as she laughed. "My intuition is not sparking today, at least not yet, but give it time. With all the witches who will be wandering around the town green today, it might."

"We haven't really talked about me finally discovering I'm a witch. But I don't understand—why doesn't Dad practice his craft like Aunt Mimi?"

Mom didn't answer right away as she finished setting out the items we would sell today. Once she was assured everything was to her satisfaction, she spoke softly. "We always thought I would grow into my powers, but I didn't. I've learned to accept that I have a strong intuition and nothing more. Your father, being a kind and wonderful husband, put aside the use of his powers for me. Reed knew I felt bad we didn't share that special gift. And for the longest time we believed you were like me. Rather than have you feel like you had missed out on something wonderful, we remained silent. It might not have been the best idea since you may have gained your powers sooner. But we can't change the past."

"Mom. Dad adores you and whatever decision he made, he did for you with an open heart. I'm not sorry I didn't find out sooner since we have no way of knowing what kind of mischief I could have gotten into being a witch at a much younger age. I don't have much control now."

"You and Nikki would have had more to talk about." She looked over my shoulder and a smile graced her lips. The one she reserved for my father.

"Don't you worry; we've never lacked for conversation." I gave her a quick hug. "Now, let's finish getting ready. Customers will soon be flocking to our booth to buy your tea and with any luck, I'll get a few people who want their leaves read."

Mom tipped her head to the side and held my hands. Her gaze burned into my soul. "Trust your instincts. They won't let you down. Above all, tell the truth on what you see. Lives will be changed today."

At a loss for words, all I could do was nod. She dropped my hands and turned to smile at Gage and Dad. The moment passed as a shiver raced down my arms. I ran my hands over them, determined to chase away the chill that had settled over me.

"I'm going to check on Milo. I'll be right back."

Gage set down the box. "Do you want company?"

I needed to spend a few minutes alone with my cat. "I'll just be a minute, but we'll touch base later."

He said, "Okay."

It was easy to see he didn't think anything was amiss. I hurried across the grass in the direction of the crosswalk when shouting from the direction of Dean Hartley's booth drew my attention, causing me to slow my steps. He was shouting, his arms gesturing wildly at a man I didn't recognize at first. He took a step back and when Dean did, I saw it was Mike Shaw. He owned the garden center on the south side of town and was a founding member of the Pembroke Cove Garden Club. Dean's face was bright red and he was shaking a fist at Mike's face. When Mike said something else, there was another angry eruption before Dean turned his back on Mike. He threw up his hands and walked away. It was good that one of the men had the sense to stop the argument. People in the town square were starting to look in their direction. I crossed the street and stepped on the brick sidewalk and withdrew the large brass key from my pocket to unlock the door to my bookshop. It was not just my business, but also my sanctuary where my familiar, Milo, hung out during the day with me and where I read my book of spells, *Practical Beginnings*.

"Milo?" I called out and checked the window seat,

which was one of his favorite places to snooze. When he wasn't there, I went in the direction of the children's corner to another one of his hidey-holes. There was my gray bundle of fur. I scooped him up, rousing him from a deep sleep.

"Hey, fur ball. Wake up. I need to ask you a question." I cradled him in my arms as I hurried to the front counter. He squirmed as I placed him down, and once seated, he began to lick his front paw, doing his best to ignore me.

"I need your advice."

"What else is new?" he grumbled as he glanced at me before going back to his grooming.

"I get the feeling something bad is going to happen today."

Finally, he stopped what he was doing and gave me his best bored look. In his deep kitty growl, he asked, "What's the problem?"

"Mom told me when I read the leaves today, to be honest about what I see. That it will change lives."

"And you decided to jump to a conclusion that it had to be bad. What has gotten into you, my dear witch?"

I crossed my arms over my chest and tapped the toe of my black pointy ankle boot. Milo could be exasperating, and why did he pick now to do so? "It wasn't what she said, but how she said it. All serious."

"Maybe someone is going to win money today or find their life partner." He rose to all four paws and did a long and lazy stretch. "This is the first year you've read tea leaves as a witch, and you read the book, right?"

I nodded.

"It doesn't mean you have the gift to do that too. So far, we can't pin down where you fit in the overall witch category. Do your best and we'll talk about it all tonight. And since you woke me from a very nice fish dream, we should have cod for dinner. And maybe ask Detective Cutie to join us."

Not bothering to keep the exasperation from my voice, I said, "Stop calling Gage that and I'll think about stopping at the dock to purchase fish." I dropped a quick kiss on his soft gray head and hurried to the door. So much for my familiar guiding me.

Business was brisk at our booth as shoppers purchased tea and a steady stream of customers wanted to sit with me as well. I had been reading tea leaves all day and so far, nothing out of the ordinary happened. I gave everyone happy things to look forward to. As the crowd was starting to thin, I leaned back in the chair and closed my eyes. I hated to admit it, but I was on the edge of exhaustion. One more hour and we could shut it down for another year. I was curious why this year had been particularly draining. Did it have anything to do with me knowing I was a witch?

A raucous commotion disturbed my break. I opened my eyes and looked around before I locked my attention on Dean Hartley's flower booth. He was having a shouting match with Tucker Gleason, the owner of the hardware store. I watched as Tucker grabbed a pair of hedge shears from Dean and shook his head in obvious disgust. Red-faced, Dean stopped shouting and handed over what looked like money to Tucker, who walked away, leaving with the tool.

As if that altercation hadn't happened, Mike Shaw approached the flower display. I braced myself for a repeat performance from Mike, but then he shook Dean's hand and clasped his other hand on top of Dean's, giving it a hearty shake as if the skirmish from earlier never happened.

As he pumped Dean's hand, he was beaming and then gestured to the blue ribbons that adorned pots of roses on display. Dean jerked his hand away and took a step back. Then he pointed in the direction of the parking area, and Mike shook his head.

I sat up straighter. This was curious. At first, it seemed they had set aside their differences. Even good friends could have a minor argument. A woman approached my table requesting a reading. Distracted, I began the process of making the tea. She drank some and then swirled the cup and turned it upside down. Another good one. I smiled as I gave her the upbeat reading—when I really longed to watch the excitement across the park.

After I had finished with my customer, commotion from Dean's booth once again broke out. This time a group of people were clustered around the roses and I could hear raised voices but not specifically what was being said. A woman, whom I recognized as Edie Jenkins, was poking him in the chest, pushing Dean back with each jab. She was a regular in my bookstore for gardening books, but I had never seen her temper before. I got up from my chair and strolled in the general direction of the group gathering in front of the flower display, in an attempt to get closer without appearing as if I was eavesdropping once I got within hearing distance of the booth. Whatever was happening over there wasn't good. Before I got close enough to hear, I saw Ava Springs, a good friend of Edie's, shouting at Dean. Alvin, Ava's brother, was lingering in the back. They were all members of the same garden club so why on earth was everyone so riled up?

"Dean," I called out. "We're going to close up soon and you mentioned you wanted to purchase some tea." Everyone stopped grumbling as I drew closer.

He gave me a confused look, and then he seemed to understand I was trying to help him get off the hot seat he was on. "Yes, thank you, Lily, for the reminder." He pushed his way through the group and escorted me back to the tea booth.

"How about a cup of tea too. Looks like you could use a pick-me-up."

He gave me a funny grin. "Maybe you should read the leaves. Everyone is talking about the great fortunes that you've bestowed on them after a reading." His grin turned into a scowl as he glanced over his shoulder. "I could use some good news right about now."

A Free Story for You

Have you enjoyed Catnaps & Crimes? Not ready to stop reading yet? If you sign up for my newsletter at www.lucin darace.com/newsletter you will received Cookies & Capers which is the start of Lily and Milo's adventure as my thank-you gift for choosing to get my newsletter.

Cookies & Capers

I stood in front of the old wood and glass door as I pocketed the keys to the Cozy Nook Bookshop. Aunt Mimi had signed her bookstore over to me. She said it felt like giving me her baby. But I loved the shop as much as my aunt did. We had worked together for the last twelve years. After attending the University of Maine, I had a degree in history and education. I had always wanted to be a teacher, but jobs were scarce and after substituting for a few years, I moved back to my hometown of Pembroke, Maine, and Aunt Mimi hired me as soon as I unpacked my suitcase.

Spending time with my aunt, learning the business, had been the best experience. I offered to buy the shop when she wanted to retire, but she wouldn't hear of it. As long as she had free books for life, and her long-term boyfriend Nate, she said it was a fair deal. From my point of view, I had built-in backup for years to come.

Now that I was the bookshop owner, Aunt Mimi was no longer coming in every day which meant her cat, Phoenix, wasn't either and the space felt empty without a kitty lying in the window or skulking about as kitties do. I was off to the Pembroke Animal Palace to see if I could find a match.

It was a short walk in the bright noonday sun. The spring air from the ocean carried a tang of salt, but the breeze was refreshing. I waved to one of my best friends, Gage Erikson, as he drove past in his police-issued sedan. My heart fluttered in my chest.

He was a detective on the force. Not that we had much crime in our small seaside town. But one of these days I was going to get brave and tell him I had been carrying a torch for him since we were in ninth grade. What's the worst thing that could happen? We'd still be best friends, right?

I continued down the brick sidewalk, waving to William North from the Sweet Spot Bakery. He was sweeping the area around the small bistro tables in front of the bakery. William was wearing a large pristine white apron and a wide smile. A deep inhale confirmed my suspicion. He was baking cookies. My mouth watered. I did a half turn and went back to where he was finishing up. "Good morning, William." I bobbed my head in the shop's direction. "What is that tantalizing smell?"

He held open the brightly polished glass door. "One of your favorites, Lily. Chocolate chip and pecan cookies. Can I interest you in one before you continue on your mission?"

I gave him a side-look. "Mission?"

He chuckled. "Over the years my Lulu had said you

had two speeds, strolling and purposeful. Just now it was purposeful so hence you're on a mission."

"I'm going to the shelter, hoping to find a kitty. The shop is lonely now that Phoenix is home every day with Aunt Mimi, and I think a cat napping in the window adds an air of serenity to the place."

"Unless you're allergic."

He had a point, but I was not willing to be deterred. I smiled. "I'm always happy to deliver to a customer." I leaned over the glass bakery case, like a kid pressing her nose against the candy case. "You made sugar cookies too and frosted them?" I sighed. I was going to need to exercise more if he continued to bake all my favorites. He was smiling at me as I looked up. "Are the chocolate pecan ready?"

He wiggled his eyebrows. "I have a tray cooling in the back."

"Then can I have one of those and a sugar cookie, but to go?"

With a flick of his wrist, he snapped open a white bakery bag and called over his shoulder. "Jerilyn, would you please bring out the last batch of cookies?"

I heard a muffled, coming, and smiled. "It's good that Jerilyn stayed on." I said nothing about his beloved wife Lulu. Rumor had it she was ill and not doing well.

He nodded. "It is. She's a hard worker and excellent with the customers."

Jerilyn bustled in from the back room carrying a large stainless-steel tray. It was lined with parchment paper and cookies the size of the palm of my hand. It was going to taste so good with a hot cup of tea later.

William put two in the bag, along with two sugar cookies, and then he handed it to me. I paid for my cookies and thanked him. "Stop by the shop later. You might just get to meet my new fur baby."

"Sounds like a plan." He grinned and crossed his arms over his rounded midsection. "You're more like your aunt than you realize. Ever since she opened that bookshop, she's had a cat, too."

I paused, tucked the bakery bag in my tote, and with my hand on the door, I turned and gave him a wide grin. "And now it's time I carry on the tradition." With a jaunty wave, I called, "Wish me luck."

Cookies & Capers is only available by signing up for my newsletter – sign up for it here at www.lucindarace.com/newsletter

Love to read?

Cozy Mystery Books
A Bookstore Cozy Mystery Series
<u>Books & Bribes</u>
It was an ordinary day until the book of Practical Magic conked Lily on the head causing her to see stars. And then she discovered her cat, Milo, could talk.

Catnaps & Crimes
The fun continues as Lily practices her magic and needs to investigate another murder.

Tea & Trouble
A fall festival and reading tea leave and just enough to propel Lily into a new murder investigation.

Scares & Dares
What does a haunted house and murder have in common? New witch Lily Michaels is determined to solve the case.

Holidays & Homicide

Love to read?

The Sandy Bay Series
<u>Sundaes on Sunday</u>
A widowed school teacher and the airline pilot whose little girl is determined to bring her daddy and the lady from the ice cream shop together for a second chance at love.

Last Man Standing/Always a Bridesmaid
<u>Barrett</u>
Has the last man standing finally met his match?

<u>Marie</u>
Career focused city girl discovers small town charm can lead to love.

Price Family Romance Series
<u>Breathe</u>
Her dream come true may be the end of his...
Crush
The first time they met was fleeting, the second time restarted her heart.
<u>Blush</u>
He's always loved her, but he left. Now he's back...the question, does she still love him?
<u>Vintage</u>
He's an unexpected distraction, she gets his engine running...
<u>Bouquet</u>
Sweet second chances for a widow and the handsome billionaire...

Holiday Romance
<u>The Sugar Plum Inn</u>
The chef and the restaurant critic are about to come face to face.

Love to read?

Last Chance Beach
<u>Shamrocks are a Girl's Best Friend</u>
Will a bit of Irish luck and a matchmaking uncle give Kelly
and Tric a chance to find love?

A Dickens Holiday Romance
<u>Holiday Heart Wishes</u>
Heartfelt wishes and holiday kisses...

<u>Holly Berries and Hockey Pucks</u>
Hockey, holidays, and a slap shot to the heart.

<u>Christmas in July</u>
She's the hometown girl with the hometown advantage.
Right?

<u>A Secret Santa Christmas</u>
Christmas isn't Holly's thing, but will a family secret help
her find the true meaning of Christmas?

It's Just Coffee Series
<u>The Matchmaker and The Marine</u>
She vowed never to love again. His career in the Marines
crushed his ability to love. Can undeniable chemistry and a
leap of faith overcome their past?

The MacLellan Sisters Trilogy
<u>Old and New</u>
An enchanted heirloom wedding dress and a letter change
three sisters lives forever as they fulfill their
grandmothers last request try on the dress.
<u>Borrowed</u>

Social Media

Follow Me on Social Media

Like my Facebook page
Join Lucinda's Heart Racer's Reader Group on Facebook
Twitter @lucindarace
Instagram @lucindraceauthor
BookBub
Goodreads
Pinterest

About the Author

Award-winning and best-selling author Lucinda Race is a lifelong fan of reading. As a young girl, she spent hours reading novels and getting lost in the fun and hope they represent. While her friends dreamed of becoming doctors and engineers, her dreams were to become a writer—a novelist.

As life twisted and turned, she found herself writing nonfiction but longed to turn to her true passion. After developing the storyline for A McKenna Family Romance, it was time to start living her dream. Her fingers practically fly over computer keys as she weaves stories of mystery and romance.

Lucinda lives with her two little dogs, a miniature long hair dachshund and a shih tzu mix rescue, in the rolling hills of western Massachusetts. When she's not at her day job, she's immersed in her fictional worlds. And if she's not writing romance or cozy mystery novels, she's reading everything she can get her hands on.